THE MARQUIS OF CARABAS

THE MARQUIS OF CARABAS

Elizabeth Brodnax

Walker and Company
New York

All the characters and events portrayed in this work are fictitious.

First published in the United States of America in 1991
by Walker Publishing Company, Inc.
Published simultaneously in Canada by Thomas Allen & Son
Canada, Limited, Markham, Ontario

Library of Congress Cataloging-in-Publication Data

Brodnax, Elizabeth.
The Marquis of Carabas / Elizabeth Brodnax.
p. cm.
ISBN 0-8027-1130-8
I. Title.
PS3552.R6225M37 1991
813'.54—dc20 90-21478
CIP

Printed in the United States of America

2 4 6 8 10 9 7 5 3 1

To Mary, for nagging,
and
to Mark, for not.

The author wishes to thank Marie Louise Brodnax, without whose knowledge of English history and the Regency genre this book would have been a lot harder to write.

PROLOGUE

THE CLASH OF steel rang through the marble corridors of the Venetian palazzo, causing those servants who heard the noise suddenly to remember urgent errands elsewhere, preferably outside the villa. If any had taken it upon himself to investigate, he would have found that the noise did indeed—as most feared—emanate from the mistress's bedroom. But none was foolhardy enough to involve himself in a situation that undoubtedly would, depending on which side one took, end by bringing the wrath of either the mistress or the master himself down upon one's head. It seemed wiser to absent oneself.

Signora della Lucca's bedroom was, as might be presumed, quite a shambles by this time. Defending the doorway with drawn rapier stood the young gentleman who, just ten minutes past, had so vociferously demanded admittance, saying that he bore an urgent message for Signora della Lucca's guest. Signora della Lucca herself was pressed against the back wall, with a strategically draped lace-edged sheet pressed to her lovely, if heaving, bosom. Her guest was hurriedly pulling on his breeches. Outside the door, the fire of red-hot rage in his eyes, was Captain della Lucca, wielding his sword with more bullish strength than finesse, and very little success.

Della Lucca was in fact discovering, to his great distress, that the gentleman blocking the entrace to his wife's boudoir was, despite his effeminate stature and looks, an expert swordsman. This realization in no way acted to soothe the injured husband's troubled breast. Uttering a cry indicative of frustrated anger, he raised his sword over his head like a sabre and attempted to force entry.

The young gentleman, however, was ready even for this unorthodox attack. A quick riposte in prime warded off the attack, and an equally subtle thrust in sexte sent della Lucca stumbling backwards, one hand clutching a bleeding shoulder.

The youth chanced a look over his shoulder. "Hurry, papa," he called impatiently, "I can't hold off this bull forever."

"I'm hurrying, I'm hurrying," said the Signora's guest rather breathlessly. "Now where are my shoes?"

"Forget the shoes, papa. And the shirt. Just go," said the young gentleman. A movement caught the corner of his eye, and he returned to his swordplay just in time to ward off della Lucca's renewed attack.

He was not at all sure how long he would hold out, for his arm was tiring under the battering force of della Lucca's rage, but at that moment a shattering of glass and a shriek from the Signora told him that his father was perhaps at last on the verge of leaving. He risked another glance at him, and caught a glimpse of a man—still agile for his fifty odd years—vaulting through the window. The young gentleman faltered and fell back in front of della Lucca's sword, performing a delicate dance around the items that littered the floor: a woman's silken nightdress, a silver mirror, a yapping spaniel that had unwisely run out from an adjoining room.

As he reached the window, his eyes narrowed in concentration. With one final, supreme effort, for his muscles were by this time screaming with pain from the exertion, he flicked della Lucca's sword from the man's enraged grip. As della Lucca scrambled to retrieve it, the youth threw his own rapier through the window, and then himself vaulted lightly through the aperture.

Landing in the alley below, he wiped his arm across his

sweaty brow. "Ah, Papa, Papa," he said ruefully. "I am getting far too old for such adventures." With that, he picked up his sword and ran lightly down the alley.

The Browns' lodgings, wherever they might be that month, were never what a fastidious person would consider fashionable, or even particularly comfortable, but then Richard Brown had not for many years been fastidious. And if his daughter Catherine occasionally sighed and wished for a little domestic comfort, well, she had never known anything else. She did upon occasion attempt to add small touches of feminine taste to their assorted resting places, but usually as soon as she had done so the Browns would find themselves once again on their travels, sometimes in the middle of the night.

Their present dwelling in Venice was similar in style to many previous ones, although in this particular case the noisome and garbage–strewn back street over which their window usually looked had been replaced by an equally noisome and garbage–strewn canal. Other than that, it was much the same as the others, consisting in this case of a small, airless room for Richard, a slightly larger but equally airless room that was shared by Catherine and Jane, the patient, practical Englishwoman whom Richard had most improbably found to care for his infant daughter over a quarter of a century previously. A third, rather more spacious room served the three of them as a sitting room, and a dark closet down the hall housed Pedro, Richard's devoted Spanish servitor and bravo. The whole was furnished with a modicum of rickety, inappropriate furniture.

It was not a particularly pleasing situation, but Catherine had learned long ago not to repine. Now, as always, she was preparing to make the best of matters. Her return from the della Lucca palazzo had been speedy. She had made the best use of the long legs God had given her to put as much distance as quickly as possible between the, she presumed, still enraged della Lucca and her own self.

However, she had not omitted to make a few sorties through some narrow back alleys in case della Lucca had managed already to put someone on her tail. She had finished by standing in the shadow of a humpbacked bridge that spanned a canal for nearly five minutes, straining her ears for any sign of pursuit. It would do neither Richard nor herself any good if della Lucca were to discover where they lived.

Upon her return, she had taken a hasty bath in the battered tin tub that Pedro obligingly and without surprise hauled in for her, then pulled on a muslin daydress. It was more than a little faded, and a sharp-eyed observer would have noticed signs of careful mending, but the Browns saved their more opulent costumes for times when their public was present. Catherine had just finished combing out her short, tawny curls when she heard the outer door open.

Sauntering out into the main room, she confronted her father, who met the level stare of her green eyes with a slightly shamefaced expression.

"So I see that you encountered no problems," she said.

"None at all," he said airily, "none at all. And I see that you too appear to have escaped unscathed."

Catherine sank down onto the shabby sofa. "Yes," she said rather shakily. "Yes, Papa. I seem to have escaped with all my limbs intact."

Drawing her long legs up under her, she rested her chin in her hands and regarded her father with a look of patient inquiry.

"So why?" she asked.

Richard turned fussily away and paced towards the window, where he stood staring out at the greasy canal. After a moment of silence, he turned back to Catherine and said querulously, "Dash it, Cat, how was I to know that her husband would return early?"

Catherine forbore from stating the obvious, that Richard should abjure the company of married women. After all, a substantial portion of their income still came from his appeal to under-appreciated middle-aged women. Instead she asked mildly, "Are we going to have to leave tonight?"

"I don't think we have to be that precipitate. Signor della Lucca is a dangerous man, of course. Anybody who is collaborating with the Austrians has to be taken seriously."

Catherine, who knew her father extremely well, refrained from asking why he had picked this dangerous man's wife to seduce. Richard never thought of such things at the right moment.

"But he's also a man of pride," Richard continued. "He is unlikely to want his name bandied around Venice, which it will be if he calls out the Guardia to arrest us. But I also think it extremely likely that I will become *persona non grata* in Venice. As will you, for that matter. We have as long as it will take della Lucca to think of a revenge that will satisfy both his anger and his pride. Which may be only a few days."

He paused, apparently struck by a sudden thought. "Catherine, how did you come to turn up at just that moment?"

"Oh, I was visiting the Contessa Veneducci—she's been quite taken with me lately, you know, and it's always worthwhile to cultivate acquaintances among the aristocracy—when someone mentioned that della Lucca's regiment had returned to Venice early. It seemed wise to warn you, so I left early, pleading a slight headache.

"Jane was out when I got back, but Pedro said that you had left for the della Lucca palazzo about an hour earlier. So I popped over, taking your rapier with me just in case—you never know what might happen, and swords are so much less messy than pistols—and mentioned to the della Lucca servants that I had an urgent message for their mistress's visitor. The rest I think you know."

"I'm in your debt for this one, Catherine."

"And the last two or three or four, Papa. How much

longer do you think I can keep this up? I swear I found gray hairs when I was brushing out my hair just now."

Richard turned back from the window, regarding his daughter with a hangdog look on his face. "I'm sorry, Cat," he said, "it's no life for a girl."

"It's no life for a woman, Papa. I'm twenty-seven. In England I'd be on the shelf already." She paused, and her ready grin lightened her face. "Of course, here in Italy I'd probably be a grandmother."

Richard's face showed his shock, then took on a look of intense calculation. "Dash it, Cat," he said finally. "Not a grandmother. Not yet."

"No," she agreed, "but getting close."

"I suppose you're right. But to return to the subject at hand, I do think that we need to leave Venice as soon as we can. But where shall we go?"

"Paris?" asked Catherine.

Richard shook his head. "The gendarmerie was rather specific just last autumn. A pity, that. The restored aristocrats are so eager to lose their newly-gained wealth."

"Madrid?"

"There was that titled gentleman you fleeced at piquet. I seem to remember that he was quite distressed."

"Yes," said Catherine, brooding.

Richard sat carefully on a rickety chair and regarded his daughter. Occasionally, at times like these, he did suffer faint pangs of conscience. While the girl had definitely been exaggerating her decrepitude, even he could not deny that at twenty-seven she should be settled and happily married. But settled was, of course, the last thing she would ever be as long as she stayed with him. If Donizetta had lived, perhaps things would have been different. But then again, he thought in a rare moment of honesty, perhaps they would not.

If only there were some way he could rescue her from this life she lived with him. Richard had never really regretted the ill-fated scheme that had made England an unhealthy place for him over thirty years before, for if it had worked he would have been rich and he liked the wandering life of an adventurer, but he did occasionally realize that Cat—despite the cool competence with which she fell in with his schemes—was not perhaps as happy as he was.

Richard was a strong believer in his own flashes of brilliance, although he usually left it to Cat to supply the practical details, so when one came to him now, he did not pause to analyze it. The girl deserved to be married. She should be married. And what's more, he decided with the chauvinism that still occasionally overcame him, even after over thirty years of being a man without a country, she needed to marry an Englishman. Nobody else would be worthy of her. Having come to this decision, the means that would be required to carry it out seemed immaterial to him. Cat would know what to do. He would leave the matter in her competent hands. But, he realized, in this one case he would have to be a little crafty, for there was, he supposed, a chance that the girl might resist.

Sighing, Catherine had placed her chin in her hands, and Richard thought once again how much she resembled the cat he named her. That tiny head set on a long, slender neck, accentuated by the close-cut Brutus crop in which she wore her dark gold hair. That creamy brown face with its wide brow and pointed chin, and its black-lashed, tip-tilted green eyes. The girl was indisputably a beauty. If he played his cards right, he was sure he could find a suitable husband for her. That suitable, to Richard, meant a man who could also support his father-in-law in style, did not worry him. It went without saying that Cat would want her father to be happy.

As if his scrutiny had disturbed her, Catherine looked up. "Istanbul?" she asked. "Cathay? Or perhaps Philadelphia? I can't think of anywhere else."

"There's always London," Richard said.

That startled her in a way that few things ever did. She

stared openly. "But you always said you could never go back. . . ."

"It's been thirty years, and I received word recently that a certain influential gentleman has died. Of course, we would not use my name."

A glimmer of excitement shone behind the cool green eyes. "Could we, Papa? Could we?" Her words tumbled over themselves. "We could settle down. I could be a governess, perhaps, and you . . . you . . ." She hesitated, as if she had lost her train of thought.

Richard shook his head. His mind had been working while she spoke, and he thought that he had come up with a way to present the matter subtly to Catherine. "No, no, Cat. Can you really see me settling down? No, if I'm to return to London it has to be in some way so special, so spectacular that I would finally get my revenge for the way they treated me. We would bedazzle my stupid countrymen with our wiles. No governessing for you. We will perpetrate a grand hoax, and you—you shall marry a nobleman and live happily ever after."

Catherine looked at him curiously. "What are you planning?"

"I have not decided yet," he said loftily, "but it will be a master stroke of genius."

"What a hand you are," she said, shaking her head at him. "You don't have the slightest notion what you plan to do. Well, you're going to have to do better than that, because I refuse to believe that the English are as stupid as you portray them. Just look at Jane."

"Jane is a ruby beyond price, a pearl among women. She has bedazzled you into believing the English are something more than they are. And she is the one who has influenced you in your ridiculous ideas. Becoming a governess, indeed! What will you say next?"

"It's not what I say next, Papa, but what you say," said Catherine firmly, refusing to be diverted from the subject under discussion. "Are you serious about London, or are you just joking? I'm not sure how we would do it, although I suppose if we were to pretend to be members of a noble Venetian family, who have decided to take advantage of the new peace to see London. . . . Or perhaps we are in trouble with the Austrians. . . . Oh, I don't know. It's all ridiculous."

"No, it's not. You could be the Marchesa Caterina, and I'll be your devoted father who has finally acceded to your demands to see Paris and London, and you will so charm the young men of England that all will fall happily in love with you. You will make one—the richest, I hope—the happiest man on earth by accepting his suit, and after the marriage perhaps it will turn out that Papa has not quite as much money as he. . . ." Richard was charmed with how well this was proceeding. The words were rolling mellifluously off his tongue. He was quite surprised when Catherine jumped up from her chair and stood threateningly over him.

"Papa, you've always used me," she cried, "but this time you're going too far. I can't believe it. You're sitting there, cold-bloodedly planning on marrying me off."

Richard's face was a study in distress. "Cat, Cat. No. No. I never meant that at all. Oh, Cat, I've been a terrible father for too many years; I just wanted to find a way to make you happy. Cat, don't be angry with me."

Her face softened. "I'm never angry with you, Papa. But I can't allow you to plan things that involve my whole life."

Richard looked relieved. "Oh, then it's simple, Cat. You'd better plan the whole affair yourself, then. You were well started before I jumped in anyway. . . . Now what, Cat?" he finished in aggrieved tones.

For, struck by uncontrollable laughter, Catherine had sunk down onto the sofa once again, and had dropped her face into her hands. "Nothing, Papa. It's all right, really it is. I'll plan the whole affair myself. Why did I ever think anything else?"

1

IT WAS EARLY enough in the evening for the street in front of Tyne House to be deserted, a fact that Mr. Alexander Carrock noted with some relief as the curricle turned the corner into Upper Grosvenor Street

"Well, thank God for that," he said to the man holding the reins of the curricle. "I appreciate your taking me up, Jerry. If I'd known the roads down from Cumberland would be so muddy, I would have started back a day earlier. I promised my grandmother faithfully that I would be here for this ball, and she would have had my hide for chair cushions if I'd turned up here after the first guests had arrived, but I didn't have the heart to fig the greys out again on such a raw day. Or Beecham either, for that matter. Not that I feel like attending a ball myself, after ten hours on the road today."

"Rather you than me at any time," his companion said. "I've never been one for doing the pretty. It beats me how you have the patience to pay court to the dowager duchess the way you do. You sure you don't want to come to that cockfight? This is sure to be a terrible squeeze, Alec, old man."

"Of course it will be," Mr. Carrock said easily, ignoring, as he always did, the remark about his attentions to his grandmother, for a strong sense of family duty made any other course unthinkable to him. "My grandmother likes them that way. But that's all right; it's sure to be one of the parties of the season. Hers always are. You go on to your cockfight, Jerry, and leave me to my own amusements."

"Well, if you're sure," his friend said, doubt still evident in his voice.

They had by this time pulled up in front of Tyne House, so Mr. Carrock jumped lightly from the curricle and waved his friend away with an amused flick of his hand.

"Fine evening, isn't it, Brothers?" he said, handing his hat and cane to the elderly butler who had advanced from the house to meet him. "How's my grandmother doing? Fretted herself into a state over my lack of punctuality yet?" Moving up the steps with Brothers, he pulled off the evening cape that he wore, revealing a navy blue, swallow-tailed evening coat of the finest Bath superfine and form-fitting white knee breeches, both of which showed off his supple, athlete's physique to advantage.

"I would not have gone so far as to put it that way, Mr. Carrock, sir," said Brothers punctiliously as he took the evening cape, "but I will say that she has been wondering. She expressed some concern to the young duchess that you might have forgotten the ball was tonight."

Mr. Carrock laughed. "I can read between the lines, Brothers. She is actually harassing everybody she can find within her megrims. I told her repeatedly before I left town that I not only knew what date her ball was but had also learned some years ago how to keep track of the days of the week. I hope she's not fussed poor Sophie half to death yet."

"The young duchess was looking a trifle worried when I came out, sir," Brothers allowed.

"Oh well, I'd better be getting upstairs quickly then," Mr. Carrock said. "Don't bother to announce me, Brothers."

As Mr. Carrock had expected, Emily Marie Verlain, Dowager Duchess of Tyne, had already taken up her position in a straight-backed gilt chair at the head of the stairs. Behind her, an anxious expression on her pretty china doll face, stood Sophronia, third Duchess of Tyne.

"Good evening, Grandmama," said Mr. Carrock lightly, dropping a kiss on her hand. "Hello, Sophie."

"Alexander," pronounced the dowager awfully. Sophie cringed visibly. "I had given up expecting you."

"I really can't think why," he said. "I told you I'd be back in time."

"Well, I know how young men can be when other amusements call them away. Anthony has not bothered to return."

The glare she cast over her shoulder at Sophie prompted that lady to launch into hurried and slightly unwise speech. "Grandmother, you mustn't blame me for that. I reminded Tony just before he left that your ball was this week. I don't think . . ."

"You never do," said the dowager sweepingly. "However, you are wrong if you believe that I hold you all responsible for Anthony's lapses. I told him before he married you that you would be a totally inappropriate wife for him."

The reasoning behind this last remark was obscure, but Sophie did not attempt to unravel it. She hung her head slightly and muttered an apology, which the dowager did not deign to answer. The interchange had apparently restored her good humor however, for she favored her grandson with a smile, although she could not refrain from one last barb.

"Well, you did make it back after all, Alexander, and I suppose I must be happy that you waste your time over an old lady's pleasure. I am fortunate in at least one of my grandsons."

Since this remark clearly maligned the absent duke, and its only possible purpose could be to upset Sophie, Alec was hard pressed to control his temper. He had, since early youth, been told repeatedly by his grandmother, who even more than his mother had been responsible for his upbringing, how lucky he was to be a Verlain, by half-blood if not by name, and perhaps because his father had died when he was barely eight years old, it had never occurred to him to dispute this statement. While he willingly and happily spent the necessary time administering to his own estates in Cumberland, he had been brought up at Tyne House, and consequently had never been able to disabuse his mind of the notion—so carefully fostered by his grandmother—that his first loyalty must always lie with the Verlains, and primarily with its self-appointed head, the dowager duchess.

He was, in fact, far more openly devoted to the dowager than his cousin, the current duke, who appeared to most, Alec included, to espouse a policy of always being where the dowager wasn't. Alec frowned upon this, for he found it irresponsible in a way inappropriate to a Verlain, but sometimes, especially when his grandmother was at her most dictatorial, he felt a great deal of sympathy for his cousin Tony.

It was just a pity, Alec thought, that Tony also saw fit to leave his wife of less than a year with his grandmother. Tony and Alec had grown up with the dowager, and presumably understood her ways, but Alec had found that little Sophie was still woefully unprepared for dealing with her. At times like this, Alec found himself close to disliking his grandmother, who was clearly determined to make sure that Sophie not be allowed to wrest away from her grand-mama-in-law one iota of the consequence she should have inherited when she married Tony.

But as Alec had been trained since earliest childhood to respect and honour his redoubtable grandmother, he said nothing of this, and the dowager's mind had apparently turned to another topic.

"I invited the Marchesa di Carabas to your ball, dear Sophronia," she informed Sophie.

Sophie acquired a look that strongly reminded Alec of a frightened rabbit—the small, fluffy kind that with a blue ribbon around its neck makes the perfect child's present.

"Do you—do you think that's wise?" she asked hesitantly. She almost never ventured to question her husband's redoubtable grandmother, but it was obvious that this latest whim of the dowager's had taken her rather aback.

The dowager drew herself up even straighter in her chair, if that were possible. "Are you questioning my right to ask whom I please, you flibbertigibbet?" she asked awfully.

"No . . . no," Sophie stammered. "You know I would never do that, ma'am." She cast a look of appeal up at Alec, who was usually her only hope of help, and saw to her relief that he showed some signs of planning to divert his grandmother.

Alec in fact was finding that his irritation was growing rather than lessening. He disliked the way his grandmother treated Sophie, and he also disliked her propensity for taking up a new favorite every Season. These were frequently women of dashing, if slightly erratic, character, who would briefly amuse the dowager with their starts. Alec felt that her championing of these damsels put the Verlains in a bad light; the dowager remained secure in the belief that it didn't matter what the common folk thought, and by common she meant anybody who did not possess the good fortune of being born or marrying a Verlain. (Alec, by virtue of his Verlain mother, just barely qualified.) Alec, through training and force of habit, had always put up with these starts, just as his uncle and aunt—Tony's parents—had before him. Tony, of course, by virtue of his frequent absences, was able mostly to ignore them. But today, for some reason, he seemed less ready to accept his grandmother's ways, perhaps because he resented her dragging Sophie into the matter.

"Is this the Italian adventuress that Gerry Comstock told me about as we drove over here?" he asked with some acerbity.

"Adventuress, fiddlesticks," said the old duchess roundly. "I've never thought much of Gerald Comstock; he wouldn't know his own head from a hole in the ground."

"That's as may be, Grandmama, but he has a keen ear for the latest gossip, and he was telling me all about this so-called marchesa just a few minutes ago. He took me up in his curricle as I was walking over from Half Moon Street. I gather that nobody really has the slightest idea if any of her claims are true. As I understand it from Jerry, she arrived suddenly, without warning or anybody's prior knowledge of her existence, barely a week ago."

The dowager turned her awful glare on Alec. "I do not think I am senile yet," she snapped.

Sophie quailed, but Alec refused to be intimidated. With a skill learned over the years, he added a little flattery. "We all know that you have been the Queen of Society for more than half a century," the dowager's frown lightened infinitesimally, "so if you signify to Society that you approve of her, which by inviting her here you have probably already done, then nobody will dare to dispute the matter. In fact, you have set your seal of approval on somebody whom you have no reason to believe is not a charlatan of the highest order. You must remember that you not only have your own reputation to think of now, but Sophie's as well." He ignored the snort of displeasure from the dowager, for during the boring ride down from Cumberland he had considered the situation and had come to some resolutions concerning Tony and his new wife. "I generally have more sense than to try and interfere with your concerns, but I wish you would at least think of Sophie before taking up with such a woman."

A spark of genuine anger had appeared in the dowager's eyes. "You can leave me to make decisions of that sort, I'll thank you, Alexander. The girl has far too much grace and breeding to be an imposter. A pert chit, perhaps, but obviously bred to the nobility. Much more than Sophronia here. I don't know why my family has such a penchant for marrying commoners."

Sophie, who was the oldest child of an impoverished baronet who had not the means to provide respectably for one daughter, let alone the six that God had seen fit to give him, mistakenly allowed herself to utter a small squeak of protest, but when the dowager turned on her she blushed furiously and hung her head.

Alec, who knew that the remark was aimed just as much at his own birth as it was at Sophie's, refused to be intimidated. He had learned from painful experience that the best approach with the dowager had always been one of fighting fire with fire. "Grandmama," he said firmly, "stick to the subject, and stop harassing poor Sophie. She doesn't have a chance against you."

"I resent that remark," said the dowager, but the hint of an impish grin crossed her face.

"So where did you meet this supposed Italian noblewoman?" Alec asked. "I presume from your remarks that you did meet her, and are not just sending out random invitations in an attempt to send Sophie and myself to early graves."

"Certainly I met her," said the dowager. "Sophronia and I were at Hookham's Lending Library yesterday, and she had come in to exchange a book. She speaks lovely English and has beautiful manners. I haven't met anyone so charming in years. I see absolutely no reason to believe that she might be an imposter."

Alec's face grew a little grimmer. "Grandmama, I can't believe that you could have been so credulous. I see absolutely no reason for an Italian noblewoman to speak lovely English or to be apparently enjoying English literature. Let alone the charm, which sounds highly suspect to me."

But with this frank speech he had evidently lost the ground he had gained earlier. The dowager's eyes filled with the icy hauteur that Sophie dreaded so. "How dare you speak to me like that, Alexander? I will not be treated in such a manner. If you have nothing better to do with yourself than make ridiculous and flippant remarks to an old woman, I can only suggest that you absent youself from this party."

Alec theatrically dropped to one knee and, raising his grandmother's hand to his lips, kissed it. "You know I don't mean anything of the sort, Grandmama," he said easily and gracefully. "I am only thinking of your best interests, and of course if you think that this woman is who she says she is, then she must be. You don't really want me to leave, do you?"

The old woman's eyes softened as she looked down at the well-muscled shoulders filling out the coat of dark blue superfine and the brown curls which covered the back of Alec's handsome head. She had always had a weakness for a handsome man, and it was impossible to remain angry with the boy when he apologized so sweetly, she thought, forgetting that the boy was now almost thirty.

"No, Alexander, of course I don't. But you should be more careful of what you say. You can be very thoughtless sometimes."

The noise of arrivals at the bottom of the stairs interrupted her.

"Lord and Lady Middleton," announced the footman, heralding the arrival of the first guests to the ball that was, despite the dowager's insistence that Sophie's name be used, her big entertainment of the Season.

The dowager's attention was diverted from the iniquities of her grandson. She adored parties, and had since she had burst onto society at the age of nineteen as the glittering, lovely young bride of the most eligible bachelor in England. When her husband had died prematurely at fifty she had continued to hold her balls and her soirees just as she always had. She had seen no reason to resign in favor of her daughter-in-law, and it is likely that not even the strongest representations would have been enough to persuade her to remove from the elegance and opulence of Tyne House, but in point of fact her beleaguered son had never dared to offer even the gentlest hint. Neither he nor his unfortunate wife had ever been able to resist her autocratic personality; in fact, there were those who said unkindly that the exhaustion of living with her was responsible for their early demise. And when her grandson had picked the unassuming, unexceptionable Sophronia Babbit as his wife, nobody, least of all Sophie herself, had seen any reason to expect that the dowager would change her ways.

So the receiving line at Tyne House was ordered as it had been for thirty years. The dowager duchess in the hostess's position—although of late she had taken to sitting in a chair—and the duchess hovering beside her, completely overshadowed by her redoubtable grandmama-in-law. Mr. Alexander Carrock, as the dowager's favored grandson, or at least the only one who had seen fit to present himself that night, stood behind her, with one hand resting lightly on the back of her chair.

The invitations had said nine o'clock, and by half-past nine the guests were trickling in. By ten the ballroom was filled with people, and it was plain to see that the dowager's ball would be, as nobody had ever doubted, the most crowded, and therefore the best, of the early Season. Mrs. Drummond-Burrell and Lady Jersey had already arrived, and there was a rumor that the Duke of Wellington himself might put in an appearance. If that was so, it would be quite a coup for the dowager, for the hero of Waterloo and the savior of Britain could not fail to make a sensation.

But one expected guest had not come, as Alex dared to point out to his grandmother. There had been a lull of some five minutes with no new arrivals when he leaned over her shoulder and whispered in her ear.

"So where is this Marchesa di Carabas, Grandmama? Not coming, do you think? Perhaps she has had second thoughts about her reception by society."

The dowager turned and eyed him awfully. "Nonsense. I am sure she will arrive very soon. If you have nothing else to do, you had better make yourself useful by fetching me a glass of brandy." The dowager had never been one to respect the dictates of society, and saw no reason to, as she put it, maudle her insides with ratafia just because it was considered a lady's drink.

"Yes, Grandmama," Alec said obediently, turning and making his way through the throng towards the room where refreshments had been laid out. He was still annoyed at the earlier contretemps and had decided that at worst the marchesa would turn out to be an ill-bred imposter bent upon using his grandmother and the entire Verlain family, and at best a hurly-burly foreigner with few manners and less idea of how to go on in London society.

He returned just in time to observe a late arrival, and while of course it could never have been said of Mr. Alexander Carrock—whom everybody knew to be a buck of the first order, a prince of society, and the dream of every young lady and her matchmaking mama both—that his jaw dropped in surprise, certainly it could be noted that his attention was fixed. Ignoring the glass of brandy in his right hand, he fumbled and found his quizzing glass with his left hand, and raised it to his eye.

The lady in question was alone. Passing through the double doors to the ballroom, she hesitated for a moment at the entrance. Some young ladies, and others not quite so young, might indeed have hesitated at the thought of confronting the whole of London society for the first time, but it was obvious in this case that the pause was for no such reason. Rather it was a conscious decision, a move calculated to give as many eyes as possible the time to notice her arrival. Alec silently applauded the consummate skill of such a move.

Sweeping his eyeglass over her, he realized that there was far more reason for applause. Her silk gown was not one of the much vaunted pastels that had graced fashion for so long, nor even a brighter jewel tone such as a daring young matron might choose to wear, but rather a dark old gold, somewhere between deep yellow and bronze, that matched exactly the color of her hair, and set off to perfection her rich, creamy skin. The only touch of color about her was the fabulous emerald necklace that sparkled at her neck, drawing attention to the exquisite curve of her bosom, a curve that was echoed at waist, hip, and thigh under the clinging silk. One slender foot, clad in a gold sandal, was thrust slightly forward, and Alec could see that the dark gold color had been carried through even to the daring paint on her toenails.

Obviously aware that she was being watched, the lady looked up at that moment and smiled—slowly, flirtatiously. The smile moved to her eyes, and Alec realized that the green of her emeralds was matched in those dark-lashed, tip-tilted eyes. Cat's eyes, he thought suddenly. The lady half turned away from him, towards the dowager, and he came to his senses to realize he had spilled a large quantity of brandy on his sleeve. Cursing under his breath with remarkable fluency, he turned away to find a servant and a napkin.

He returned to find that the dowager was regarding him with suppressed amusement, and realized that she had seen everything.

"Who was that?" he asked, although he already knew the answer. He was unable to keep a note of irritation from his voice, which ended up annoying him even further.

"The Marchesa Caterina di Carabas," she replied triumphantly.

2

DESPITE HER DRAMATIC entrance, the Marchesa might perhaps have lacked for partners, for London society was notoriously suspicious of outsiders, especially foreign outsiders, if the dowager had not made sure that she was presented to those who mattered. After the marchesa had been seen talking with animation to both Lady Jersey and Mrs. Drummond-Burrell, and dancing with several gentlemen of the highest consequence, she could barely find a minute to call her own. She was the sensation of the evening, and it did not seem too early to say that she bade fair to be the sensation of the Season.

It could be seen that the marchesa danced with grace and ease, even the waltz, and for once there were none who dared murmur that she had not yet been given permission by one of the Patronesses of Almacks. Lady Jersey was standing with Mrs. Drummond-Burrell when the marchesa swung lightly into the first waltz, and when that second lady, who was known for her frosty insistence on the correct forms, raised one eyebrow, Sally Jersey merely laughed.

"Who are we to say what she can or cannot do, my dear?" she said lightly. "No doubt the girl has been waltzing in Rome, or wherever it is she comes from—I believe it is actually Venice—for years."

"She's not young, that I will allow," said Mrs. Drummond-Burrell. "But not married, I gather."

"No," said Lady Jersey. "She tells me she was engaged

at seventeen to a young man of the Italian nobility, who was killed fighting against Napoleon. She has been unable to find his match since then, and so has remained unwed."

"A likely story," Mrs. Drummond-Burrell sniffed, but Lady Jersey merely smiled, watching the queenly grace with which the young woman performed the steps of the waltz.

Mr. Carrock had not intended to ask the marchesa to dance. To be strictly accurate about the matter, he did not think that he had ever actually done so. He had made the mistake of approaching his grandmother when she was talking to the lady in question, and in retrospect it was clear to him that this had been folly of the highest order. He, at least, no matter what idiocies his grandmother might stoop to, had not meant to dignify the lady's pretensions with an appearance of approval.

There is little, however, that a man can do, when fixed with his grandmother's beady eye and informed that this is his dance.

"Come to collect your waltz, have you, Alexander?" the dowager inquired affably. "The marchesa was just telling me that she was sitting this one out, and I told her that you had been waiting all evening for such a chance."

Faced with the inevitable, Alec bowed with polished form.

"Marchesa?" he asked.

"I would be delighted," she said in a quiet but assured voice. He noticed that while she had no trace of an accent, she pronounced each word with a musical lyricism that gave a touch of exoticism to her speech.

With a smile, she placed one gloved hand lightly on his arm and allowed him to lead her out onto the floor.

The first few minutes of the dance were accomplished in silence. The marchesa seemed content to enjoy the rhythm and steps of the dance, and Alec was battling conflicting emotions.

His annoyance with his grandmother had not yet had a chance to diminish, and he did not feel that there was necessarily any reason why it should. While there was no denying that the old lady remained as sharp as a whistle, she was indisputably becoming more outrageous every year. Alec also sometimes wondered if this year she wasn't acting in part out of pique and a dislike of Sophie.

Whenever the thought presented itself to him, he would try to put it out of his head, for it was hard to suspect such wanton cruelty from the woman who had to a great extent brought him up, but he had to admit that she was riding Sophie very hard. He thought he detected a streak of jealousy there, and there was definitely some sort of determination not to allow Sophie to hold the position that was hers by rights.

The same had been true of his grandmother's relationship with his Aunt Maria, of course, but that had somehow been different. He had not been born during the years when presumably the dowager had been demonstrating with all the vigor necessary for a complete victory her innate superiority over her daughter-in-law, and his relationship with his subdued, withdrawn Aunt Maria had always been that of a child to an adult. Sophie was different. He hated the thought of her shy charm extinguished by his grandmother's overpowering personality.

And he did think that an attempt to distress Sophie was probably behind the dowager's championship of the glamorous marchesa, who was so clearly everything that Sophie was not. He had been prepared to dislike the Italian woman from the moment he heard of her, and now that he had seen her he should be disliking her even more.

But he had not been prepared to find himself overwhelmed by the feel of the marchesa's supple body resting so lightly but so intimately within the circle of his arms.

He was not a man who had generally found much pleasure in the women that Society arrayed so generously before him. The milk-and-water misses, each eagerly anticipating the possibility that he might bestow upon her the honor of his coveted name in marriage, bored him. The fashionable young matrons, who had frequently made it abundantly clear that they would be happy to enliven his nights, repelled him. He was in fact, at nearly thirty, apparently unlikely to indulge in a liaison of any kind—whether wedded or otherwise.

He saw no need to marry. As he cheerfully pointed out to any acquaintance who twitted him on the subject, there was no title to pass on, and his cousin, who had already produced three promising young sons, would inherit his considerable wealth and lands.

His lack of interest in the women who would so willingly have become his mistress was another matter altogether. He was not by any means a monk, but he was noted among his associates for ignoring both the society matrons who angled for his attentions and the charming barques of frailty who would have loved to have bestowed their exclusive attention on him in return for the material advantages he could give them.

Gerry Comstock, who was as close to an intimate friend as he possessed, although he had many acquaintances with whom he spent entertaining evenings, had told him more than once that he was hag-ridden. He had denied the accusation vehemently, but it held a certain truth. Although his mother had died some four years previously, there were too many women in his life already. His grandmother equalled two or three at least, and of late Sophie had increased the menage. Tony, of course, should have been the one to deal with Sophie, but Tony seemed reluctant to do so.

The truth of the matter was, although he did not completely realize it, that he just did not have the emotional resilience to add yet another woman to a life already cluttered with the feminine presence. An emotional attachment of the sort that was required if he ever became involved with a woman on a long-term basis just did not appeal to him, and he had known this for years.

So why did he feel stirrings of interest in this supposed marchesa, this scandalous foreign female whose friendship with his grandmother was undoubtedly going to cause him problems by the handful. Why, when he held her in his arms, did he feel such an unaccustomed sense of excitement, as if he were about to chart new and fabulous territory? He glanced down at the top of her tawny curls, and his eyes without volition followed the line down to her creamy bosom and the fabulous diamond-set emeralds which enhanced it to such perfection.

"Family jewels, marchesa?" he asked sardonically, in an attempt to ward off the other thoughts that were willy-nilly attacking him.

"Pardon me?" she asked, with a sweeping glance upwards of her tiptilted, black-lashed green eyes.

"Your emeralds are amazing. I have never seen anything quite like them."

"They are beautiful, are they not? And yes, they have been in my family for many generations. It is told that one of my ancestors bought them from Messer Marco Polo, who had brought them back from China."

"The setting looks modern," he said skeptically.

"My grandfather had them reset for his bride. A pity, I think, but I have seen portraits with the old setting, and I do not think I could have worn them. It was very heavy, with a lot of gold. The diamonds were my grandfather's addition."

"You are from Rome, I believe, Marchesa?"

She looked surprised. "Ah, no, from Venezia, from . . . from Venice."

"And your family is obviously an old one there, if you speak of Marco Polo with such familiarity."

"Very old, although of late we have withdrawn some from the public eye. It has been traditional for the di Carabasi to be Senators of Venice, even to be elected to the

Council of Three, but in these troublous times of war, such things have changed." Her face, which had been so open and alive, clouded over.

Alec remembered that there had been talk of a fiancé killed during the wars with Napoleon, and wondered if that was of what she thought. Suddenly, he felt slightly ill-at-ease, as if he had uncovered some private matter with his probing questions. He wondered what he should say.

But the cloud that had passed over the marchesa's face left as quickly as it had come. "That is something of which we do not need to talk. I am so happy to be here in England, and when my father comes to join me, ah, then my happiness will be complete."

"Your father will be joining you soon?"

"Yes. There were business matters that had to be finished before he could leave Italy, but I was so impatient to see the English Season that I insisted I must come ahead. I expect him within the month."

"And your mother?"

"Ah, no. She died many years ago. It is a pity, for she would have enjoyed the chance to revisit the country where she spent some happy years as a child. She came to school here as a young girl. She loved the country, and insisted that I speak English with her often."

"So that is why you speak our language so beautifully."

She smiled, and the brilliance of her expression ravished him. "Thank you," she said. "It is very kind of you to say so."

Alec was nonplussed. He had wanted to dislike this woman, had even been prepared if need be to denounce her as a fraud, but placed face to face with her himself, he was forced to admit that not only was she completely charming, but that everything about her seemed to shout of openness and honesty. Her manners were exquisite, and if her bearing was perhaps a little more forward then he would have liked associated with his grandmother and Sophie, she was certainly a vast improvement over a number of previous examples. But he could not like his own reaction to her. It made him feel as foolish as his grandmother, and he did not like feeling foolish. He wished he had not allowed himself to be pushed into this dance. He wished the dance would never end. Sighing, he unconsciously held the marchesa a little more tightly than propriety would strictly dictate. She glanced up at him with tilted emerald-green eyes, but said nothing.

"Jane, Jane, I'm back."

The call that echoed through the corridors of the London town house was uttered in a way far more suitable to an adolescent schoolboy than a lady of twenty-seven, especially one who was supposed to be in the process of convincing London society that she was the cream of Italian nobility. With a sigh, Jane Verne, who was sitting in Catherine's bedroom painstakingly adding rows of blond floss to a blush-rose muslin walking dress, stuck her needle carefully in the cloth.

The door flew open, and Miss Catherine Brown, or the Marchesa di Carabas, as she was currently to be called, hurtled through, her expensive Chinese silk shawl falling unnoticed to the floor behind her.

"It worked, Jane!"

Jane looked fondly at the young woman she had been a mother to since the day that Richard Brown, a desperate man with a starving two-month-old child and a dying wife, had hired her as a wet nurse, back in those terrible months following the fall of the Bastille. She smiled in response to Catherine's enthusiasm, but lifted a finger to her lips.

"I sent your abigail to bed, Catherine, but you don't want to wake her up."

Catherine sobered for a moment, picking up the shawl and closing the door carefully behind her, but a moment later she was waltzing around the room, although now her exuberance was displayed in a quieter fashion.

"They believed me, Jane. There can be no question. I

thought I had played the game fairly well at Hookham's with the Dowager Duchess of Tyne, but I was a sensation tonight."

She swooped down to give Jane a hug, then danced away again, casually detaching the emerald necklace which glittered around her neck as she did so. Giving the necklace a flick that sent it flying across the room to land in a pile of green and gold fire in the center of the carpet, she flung herself flat across her bed.

"Catherine," Jane said sharply, "pick that up."

"Why? It's only paste, Janey, my Jane."

Jane laid the sewing aside and stood up. "Catherine," she said firmly, "I have humored your father in every ridiculous whim he has indulged in for twenty-seven years, but I am only going along with this present truly terrifying escapade if you behave yourself in a sane and sensible manner. You know the necklace is only paste, and I know it's only paste, but your abigail does not."

Stooping, she picked up the necklace, then placed it carefully in the velvet case that lay open on the dressing table. The frown fading from her face, she walked over to the bed and stood looking down at Catherine.

"Oh, Catherine, my darling, were you really a success?"

Catherine's eyes sparkled. "Oh, Jane, I was a sensation. You wouldn't believe. The dowager duchess adores me, and even Lady Jersey and Mrs. Drummond-Burrell were impressed. I have already received a promise of vouchers for Almack's from Lady Jersey, and any number of perfectly charming ladies and—" she smiled "—even more charming gentlemen have promised to call on me."

Sitting up, she started to untie the silken ribbons that fastened her Grecian sandals at the ankle. But now her jubilation faded, to be replaced by a look of serious concentration.

"In fact, they all adored me. Except perhaps a certain Mr. Alexander Carrock, who did appear to view me with some suspicion."

Jane sat down on the bed, a look of alarm crossing her normally placid face. "Heavens, Catherine, do you know why?"

Catherine was struggling with the knot on her second sandal, which seemed to have become hopelessly entangled. "I think it might be just on principle. There didn't seem to be any one thing in particular that bothered him, although he questioned me rather more closely than anyone else has bothered to do. He seems to be generally just a most suspicious gentleman, although the fact that he is the dowager duchess's grandson may have something to do with it. Perhaps he fears that I am trying to insinuate myself into her good graces. He's right, of course, I am."

Giving up on the knot, she flung herself back down on the bed, throwing her hands in the air as she did so. "Oh, I don't know. Maybe he's just an unusually suspicious type." A sly smile crossed her face. "He's extremely attractive, however. Broad shoulders that fill out his coat—obviously no need for padding there—slim hips and very good legs. And an absolutely dazzling smile."

"Anyway, he avoided me for most of the evening, other than staring at me quite terribly when I first arrived, and then finally only danced with me because his grandmother made him. He asked me all sorts of questions about Venice, but I think I managed to satisfy him. You should have heard the rigmarole I spun about the necklace. A family heirloom, I said, passed on to me by my grandmother. God bless that little shop in Paris, Jane. They do the most amazing work. Whatever else anyone sees fit to question, I don't think there's a chance they'd feel even a single doubt about that necklace."

She yawned. "Oh, Jane, I'm suddenly so very tired. Would you pretend I'm five years old again and help me undress? I can't get this stupid knot out at all."

With her customary efficiency, Jane soon had the knot untied, the dress off, and Catherine tucked cozily into bed. She bustled around the room, smoothing the wrinkles out of the gold silk as she hung it in the closet, and placing the emerald necklace with the other jewelry in a little cubby-hole under the windowsill. Catherine watched her through half-closed eyes, feeling her normal comfortable sense that wherever Jane was, the world would somehow continue to revolve in its same steady course.

Dear Jane, she thought drowsily, how does she keep up with us? She thought of Jane perched on a tiny donkey during those six months they had spent with a band of guerilleros in Spain, often only half-a-step ahead of the French. That had been one of the many times that Catherine had spent dressed as a boy, although it was the last time she had tried it for an extended period of time, for what had been natural and easy at thirteen or fourteen had become a challenge to accomplish at twenty-three, and it had only been Jane's watchful vigilance that had kept her from disaster.

Catherine's eyes drifted closed, but she sensed that Jane had blown out the candles and left the room. I wonder where Papa is right now? she thought dreamily. This prank, like all the others, was performed at her father's instigation, but for the first time he was not at her side, carrying it through with her. He was not always a help, for his fits and starts had landed them in as many scrapes as his brilliant ideas had saved them from, but she missed the company and the support. She wished he could be with her from the start in what had to be their most daring escapade, but she understood the impossibility of that.

Many, many years ago, long before Catherine had even been born, Richard Brown had done something that had made his presence in England a strong liability. Apparently, it was only now, with the worst of his enemies dead of a ripe old age, that he could consider the possibility of a return. But it had to be done carefully, in a circumspect fashion. If he arrived in England, merely announcing that he was the Marquis of Carabas, whom nobody had ever heard of, there was always the chance that somebody would dig into the depths of memory and remember the young trickster Richard Brown, who had fled the country nearly thirty years before. But if the lovely young marchesa, who benefited nearly as much from her youth and beauty as from the fact that nobody in England had ever seen her, was to come before him, preparing the way, readying people's minds. . . .

Catherine was nearly asleep, but her own mind, in that strange unfocused way it has between waking and dreaming, continued to wander. It was lucky, she thought, that they had been so flush right before the debacle in Venice. Signora della Lucca had been a generous mistress before her husband's inopportune return. With careful husbanding, Catherine thought she could make the money last for nearly two months, and by then Richard would have come, and Richard had an uncanny skill with dice.

And what then? she wondered. She knew what Richard hoped, but feared he was, as he had often done before, fooling himself. Even if they were completely accepted as scions of Italian nobility, feted and lauded in London society, was there really any chance that she would net herself a husband? If that *was* what she desired.

Discounting as negligible the concentrated power of her own charm, which Richard had seen so clearly, Catherine thought it unlikely. These insular English might be willing to dance and dine with an Italian noblewoman, but she thought there was little chance that one would actually wish to marry her. And if one did, what then. Richard seemed to think such an offer would solve all their problems. Catherine rather thought it would create a whole new set. Was it really possible to pretend to one's own husband all one's life?

Well, there was not much point in worrying so far into the future; she had learnt that many years before, at an age when most small girls were still cradling their dolls.

You took life one step at a time, one step at a time, and you waited to see what would come, because only then would you know what to do . . .

3

"HELLO, SOPHIE. Run and get your hat and gloves. I've come to take you for a drive in the park," Alec said.

The dowager, who had been sitting with Sophie in the small drawing room, a pleasant apartment filled with spring sunshine that faced south across Upper Grosvenor Street, sniffed. "I suppose it didn't occur to you to ask if it was agreeable with me, Alexander," she said. "Sophie and I might have had plans, you know."

"Do you, Soph?" Alec asked.

Sophie hesitated, looking with doubt in her wide eyes from the dowager to Alec and back again. "Well, I don't . . . nothing was planned . . . at least I thought you were going to. . . . Do you need me, ma'am?"

"Of course she doesn't," said Alec. "Come on, Grandmama. It's a beautiful day and Sophie needs the fresh air. She doesn't get out often enough."

"I suppose you couldn't have asked your old grandmother."

"You don't like driving with me. You say that I'm a young whippersnapper and that my curricle is a hurly-burly affair you wouldn't be seen dead in, and then you spend the whole time criticizing my driving into the bargain. Besides, old Lord Greville was saying at the club that you were going driving with him this afternoon. That's what gave me the idea of taking Sophie out."

Rolled up on all sides, the dowager had to concede defeat.

"Go and get your hat and gloves, girl," she barked at Sophie. "What are you waiting for?"

Sophie fled.

"Do you have to be so harsh on her?" Alec asked mildly as the door closed behind her.

"Fiddlesticks," said the dowager. "You don't know what you're talking about. The girl's a silly chit. If she just had an ounce of gumption. Can't think why Anthony ever married her."

"But he did, and she is what she is. I wish you'd save your fidgets for me."

"Don't you order *me* about, boy. I knew what I was doing long before you were even born."

And that, thought Alec, was undoubtedly true. He changed the subject, since there was obviously no point in continuing in this vein.

Sophie reappeared in short order arrayed in bonnet, pelisse, and gloves, and Alec whisked her away before the dowager had a chance to make any more snappish remarks. The day was brisk, but bright with spring sunshine, and they were not the only ones to venture out for a drive or walk in the park. In between waving at acquaintances, Alec and Sophie chatted easily. Nobody had ever accused Sophie of being a bluestocking, but she had pretty manners, and could hold her own end in a conversation if given half a chance. Alec reflected that she would make a perfectly good wife for Tony, who was not at all bookish either, if Tony would refrain from dashing off at the slightest provocation.

He smiled down at Sophie. "How did things go while I was out of town? Any word from Tony? Will he be back from Newmarket soon?"

Her smile faded slightly. "I don't know. I haven't heard a thing from him. I had hoped he would write at least."

"Tony's never been great shakes at things like writing. I wouldn't take it personally if I were you," Alec said kindly.

She shook her head. "Your grandmother says that if I

were the right wife for Tony, I'd keep him by my side," she said in a non-committal voice that dared him to guess whether or not she cared about this opinion.

Alec considered what he should say. He had spent some time deliberating on this matter during the trip down from the North, had in fact invited Sophie to drive with him precisely so he could attempt to gauge her frame of mind.

He found that he worried about the chit. When Tony had announced his engagement last year, he had been surprised but not unduly so. While Tony had been only twenty-four, it was a given that he needed an heir for the dukedom. It was only a matter of time until he did marry. And Alec had rather suspected that the marriage was a love match. Sophie was an appealing child; it wouldn't have surprised Alec at all if Tony had fallen head over heels in love with her. There certainly had been no other reason for the match. Sophie was not wealthy, and there were few families that could claim birth to equal the Verlains.

But that belief had come before Tony had gone off to the Shires for the hunting, leaving Sophie with the dowager at Tyne. And Christmas at Tyne had been a truly dismal affair, with Tony apparently neither willing to take his bride of six months off alone, as might have been expected, or to protect her from his grandmother. Sophie had alternated between spells of shy withdrawal whenever the dowager was present and fits of sparkling but strained gaiety in the older woman's absence.

He had not known Sophie well when she had been a debutante, but while she had always appeared a slightly empty-headed little thing, she had also always seemed quite happy. Nobody else seemed to notice, but he thought the opposite was definitely true now. And since Tony was clearly unwilling to do anything, this meant, Alec had decided, that he had to do something about the matter himself.

But what the hell was he supposed to do?

"Well, I wouldn't worry about comments like that if I

were you," he said heartily, thinking that he sounded like a fool. Of course she worried about comments like that. With Tony acting as if he wished he'd never encumbered himself with a wife, and their grandmother apparently trying to make Sophie take all the blame, it was no wonder if she often seemed a little blue.

"I suppose so," she said, and he thought there was a note of despondency in her voice.

"Are you happy?" he asked, and then cursed himself. He was certain she wasn't happy.

Sophie turned her face away. "Of course I'm fine," she said, and laughed a little. The laughter was forced, but there was nothing much Alec could say.

They drove in silence for several minutes before Sophie opened the conversation again. "I know you didn't approve of Grandmother inviting the Marchesa di Carabas to her ball, and I did agree with you at the time. But, you know, I think she's rather nice. She came over and talked to me for quite a while, because she said the dancing had quite tired her out."

"Really?" said Alec, surprised. He hadn't noticed that, and hadn't thought the marchesa the type to waste her time being kind to other women. He could cynically have said that it was only Sophie's social connections that had made her attractive, but he knew perfectly well that the marchesa would have been far better served chatting up his grandmother if that were her aim.

"Oh, yes. She told me quite a lot about Venice. It sounds like a lovely place. Maybe Tony will take me there, although perhaps not because the marchesa says they don't have many horses there. Because of the canals, you know."

"Well," said Alec, and would have said more, but Sophie once she started chattering was not easy to stop.

"She's going to Lady Harrington's *al fresco* party, she told me. I was glad to hear that. Perhaps I'll have a chance to talk with her there, as well. Are you going, Alec?"

"I hadn't planned on it.

"Oh, do come, please. It would please Grandmother." Unspoken was the implication that things that pleased the dowager made life considerably easier for Sophie.

Alec knew that, and was also conscious of a certain interest in seeing the marchesa again. Perhaps he had been wrong to be so suspicious of her. She must at least have a good heart. Certainly it would harm nothing to speak and perhaps walk with her a little.

"If you like," he said, smiling down at Sophie's eager little face, and was rewarded by a smile of real pleasure.

"The white muslin, I think, and with that the bergere straw hat with the pale pink ribbons," Jane said decisively.

Catherine pondered this a moment, then nodded in agreement. "You're absolutely right. In fact, it's a master stroke. *Très simple*, *très chic*, just right for a cold collation and a little daffodil viewing in the country. And so different from anything that I've worn up until now. That will keep them guessing."

She got up from the bed and kissed Jane on the cheek. "Now run along and pick something for yourself, Janey. I'm so glad you've agreed to come."

"Well, I think it's only right to remind them that you're not alone in the world. I'm not going to accompany you to the balls—I'm much too old and never did know a thing about that—but I think a little afternoon excursion would be just right."

"Oh, absolutely, although I have an idea that what Lady Harrington means by a simple afternoon picnic *al fresco* may not be as little as all that. Everybody I've met has admitted to planning to go. The squeeze of the season will be more like it, I think."

"And do you think that your Mr. Alexander Carrock will be attending?" asked Jane. "I'm interested in seeing for myself the only gentleman in town who seems to have caught your attention. Certainly I haven't heard half as much about those sprigs of fashion who have been thronging our drawing room for the last ten days as I did about one dance with a certain person."

Surprisingly, Catherine flushed slightly. "He has not caught my attention. I was merely worried that he might suspect me. It's vital that I remain on good terms with his grandmother if I want to succeed, and he seems to have her ear. Let alone the fact that he could do a great deal of damage himself if he ever decided to take an active distrust against me. But as he has apparently made no further effort either to see me or to discourage her from doing so, I think that at the moment it's merely guarded suspicion."

Jane laughed and agreed, but her calm grey eyes scanned Catherine's face, as if looking for some sign that she didn't find. "Well, I'm off to dress," she said lightly. "Shall I call your abigail on the way? I don't know why we pay her such shocking wages when you end up doing all the work yourself, Cat."

"I can't get used to standing like a block of wood while somebody other than you does up my buttons for me. But think what a scandal it would be if I didn't have one. Yes, tell her to come on up. I think the muslin might be pressed to advantage, anyway."

Catherine had turned away, and was standing by the window, staring out into the street. Jane regarded her back for a moment longer with a puzzled look, then turned and left the room, closing the door softly behind her.

After much discussion and a close perusal of numerous calculations, Catherine had decided that the di Carabas household would not expend the effort on setting up a carriage for the short time that she planned to stay in London.

"Just too much trouble," the marchesa explained when asked. "Perhaps when my father joins us he will feel differently, for men often have their own views on such matters. But for myself, I feel that the house is enough responsibility. I have no desire to take on a carriage, two horses, a coachman, a groom." She flung her hands in the air in a typically Italian fashion. "I would much rather spend my time enjoying myself than with such worries."

Or, as Catherine said to Jane in the privacy of the hackney that was taking them out to Richmond. "I just don't see how I can squeeze that out of what I have for us to live on. The house is such a drain, but we have to have a house, even if we are dreadfully understaffed. As for that, I suppose I'm giving Italy a reputation for being shockingly hard on servants. It's really terrible how much I expect our poor people to do. But I can *not* afford to pay the wages on another housemaid."

Well, at least there's Teresa," Jane pointed out, seeing that Catherine seemed about to sink into agonies of worry over money again. "I'm glad we're able to pay her fairly well, for she does the work of ten. I don't think she even knows she's supposed to have two kitchen maids and a scullery maid to order around."

"Oh, Teresa is a godsend. She's so pathetically grateful to you, Jane, for taking her in when she came to the back door like that, that I honestly think she'd work for no wages at all. To have us to talk Italian to, when she thought she'd been marooned forever in a country where nobody knew a civilized language. And you know, we may yet cast the reputation of the dowager's French chef in the shade with the splendor of her ravioli. Perhaps I'll have a dinner party soon to show her off."

The hackney, which had been jolting over increasingly bumpy roads since leaving the post road some fifteen minutes previously, swung through the stone pillars of an estate gateway and turned up a driveway lined with rhododendrons, which were just starting to show the first glimpses of color in their buds. After a little less than half a mile they rounded a corner and came upon the sweep which fronted the house. It was a modern house, built within the last thirty years, and of pleasing aspect, with its graceful lines, tall windows, and golden stonework. On the other side of the sweep, the park fell away in close-clipped lawns to a small artificial lake with several islands joined by wooden bridges at its center. And, as Lady Harrington had promised, everywhere there was a profusion of daffodils, in varying shades of gold, yellow, and white. The weather, as it had often been of late, was fitful, but when the sun shone through the clouds it was a pleasing sight.

But while the eye might be briefly charmed by this view of sylvan serenity, it was perforce caught and held by the frenzy of activity that was evident on the carriage sweep and nearer lawns. Catherine and Jane were by no means the first to arrive, and the scene was one of ordered chaos—of carriages, ranging from travelling coaches to curricles to phaetons, pulling up and unloading passengers and then continuing on around the sweep, presumably to stables at the rear; of ladies in all styles of elegant muslin walking dresses, some wearing bonnets, some chip straw hats, some sporting delicate and useless parasols; of gentlemen in their skin-tight pantaloons and extravagantly shined Hessian boots. Most were clustered in groups near the sweep, but some had started to move away in pairs and trios to admire the daffodils and feed the swans that swam on the lake.

"You see," said Catherine, "not quite the simple picnic that Lady Harrington promised us, but then, were you really expecting it?"

"Not after what you told me, my dear," Jane said mildly. "Here," she added, seeing that the hackney had pulled up and Catherine was preparing to climb down, "take this shawl. You're going to need it in that thin dress." She handed over the lacy cashmere shawl that she had been carrying on her lap. "I, thank God, being your chaperon and seeing no need to dress in the height of fashion, will be quite warm enough in my pelisse. But despite the daffodils, I think you will find it quite chilly when the sun is behind the clouds."

"Yes," said Catherine a little ruefully. "It's not quite

Italy, is it? Although Venice can be quite icy when the wind whips down from the Alps."

She took the shawl and, draping it carefully around her shoulders so that it fell in elegant folds, gave her hand to one of Lady Harrington's attending footmen and stepped down from the carriage.

Turning back to Jane, who was being assisted from the carriage after her, she said meditatively, "I suppose we should tell the driver to stay."

"If you wish to send him back to London, Marchesa, I think that my grandmother could find a place for your companion in her landaulet, and I would be charmed to give you a ride home in my curricle," said a voice behind her.

Startled, Catherine turned to find Mr. Carrock regarding her.

"Why, that would be truly delightful," she said warmly. "A hackney is merely a conveyance, while with you I would have not only the pleasure of a ride in a fine carriage, but also the enjoyment of your company."

"We'll consider it settled, then," he said. "Would you care to take a stroll around the garden with me."

"Thank you, sir. It would be a pleasure. Let me just pay off the hackney, and then my dear Jane and I would delighted to join you."

She thought his face fell slightly, and her heart took a sudden, incomprehensible leap, but before she could reply, Jane stepped in.

"I have not had the pleasure of meeting you, sir, but from what Catherine has told me I think you must be Mr. Carrock. I would far prefer to find a comfortable seat with perhaps a cup of tea, and let you younger people indulge in your exercise alone."

"Oh, my manners have been lacking," Catherine said with a blush. What was it about this gentleman, she wondered, that seemed to addle her wits whenever she was in the vicinity? "Jane, as you have correctly speculated, this is Mr. Carrock, whom I met at the Duchess of Tyne's ball. He is the Dowager Duchess's grandson, I believe. Mr. Carrock, this is my dear companion Miss Jane Verne."

Jane held out her hand, and Mr. Carrock bowed very correctly over it. The formalities having been dispensed with, they paid off the driver with all due dispatch. Once Lady Harrington had been found and respects paid to her, they were able to locate a pleasant seat with a view of the lake for Jane, who professed herself to be quite comfortable to sit in the sun and enjoy the spectacle.

Catherine set her hand on Mr. Carrock's arm, and they strolled off together.

"This is a novel thing to me, your English spring," Catherine said. "Jane has told me often about it, but I don't think that anything can rival the reality. When we drove up from Dover a month ago, there was just the barest fuzz of green leaves on the trees, and now look at it. Leaves out all over the place, and everywhere you look a bird singing or a daffodil blooming. Even in London I am constantly amazed."

He smiled. "So you like it. I would have thought that you, from the city of romance, with your canals and your gondolas, your history, would not have seen so much to delight in here in England."

"I have grown up on stories since I was a child. My mother, I think I told you, came to school here. She met my dear Miss Verne there, for Jane was a teacher in the school, and insisted that she come back to Italy with her, for she was fearful of the arranged marriage she returned to, and wished a friend. She was in fact very happy, I believe, but the wars came and it was difficult for Jane to return here, so she stayed. She had no family here, no reason to come back, so even when my mother died she stayed to care for me, for which I shall be always eternally grateful. But can you wonder that between the two of them they instilled in me a wish to see *la bella Inghilterra*?"

Catherine stopped, bewildered by the flow of conversation that she had launched upon. There seemed to be something about this man which encouraged her to be seen at her sparkling best, and while there was much in her discourse that was total fiction, there was also something of the truth, which disconcerted her. Jane *had* instilled in her a desire to see the homeland she had never known, and she had never confided that to anybody other than Jane before, for she would not have wanted to hurt her father.

She realized that Mr. Carrock was smiling down at her, and she smiled in reply. It was a pleasure to walk with a man who topped her by some inches, for at five foot seven she was a tall woman, and while that had on numerous occasions been an advantage to her, it meant that she was often of a height with the men she met. It was, in fact, a pleasure to walk this way with a man at all, for, despite her chequered career, this game of flirtation between man and woman was not one she had often tried. The fringes of society which the Browns inhabited had not often thrown up situations like this London escapade, where she could trust the men she met enough to let down her guard in such a way. Alec Carrock's arm was warm under her hand, and the intimacy pleased her.

"Shall we stroll down to the lake?" he asked her. "I am told that the islands are pretty."

"It sounds charming," she said.

They paced together across the grass, he asking her with obvious and genuine interest about life in Italy, she sketching in with a vivid brush a story of a motherless childhood in an echoing Venetian palazzo, with a father she had adored who had spoiled her outrageously, and her beloved Jane who had made sure that she never learned to capitalize on her father's lenience. It was a lie, and yet so much of it was true, and she found herself thrilling to his enthusiasm.

They reached the first of the bridges, and walked across, pausing to admire the swans that sailed serenely across the mirrored surface of the lake. The island, when reached, was far more isolated than the lawn had been. They could still hear the chatter of voices echoing from the other islands and the shore, but rather than an open lawn, they were walking on narrow paths winding through the rhododendron bushes, paths that would suddenly open out for a moment into secluded nooks furnished with marble benches.

"A perfect spot for a tryst," remarked Alec Carrock with a smile.

"Yes," said Catherine, but distractedly, for she had thought she heard somebody crying.

She listened, and heard the noise again.

"Do you hear something, Mr. Carrock," she asked.

He looked puzzled, and had started to reply in the negative when he paused himself.

"Yes," he said.

At that moment a tiny, drooping figure in a chip straw hat rounded the corner, dabbing ineffectually at tears with a tiny gossamer handkerchief.

"Sophie!" exclaimed Alec.

4

SOPHIE PAUSED, MADE as if to turn back the way she had come, then apparently realized that flight was unlikely to help.

"Hello, Alec," she said, in what was obviously a valiant attempt to appear at ease.

"Sophie, what's wrong?" he asked, reaching her side with a few, quick strides.

"N–nothing."

"Balderdash. People don't wander around crying for no reason at all, Sophie. Even I know that."

Sophie ignored this attempt at humor. "Well, I do," she said defiantly.

"Sophie, there's clearly something wrong. Can't you tell me what it is?"

Sophie cringed, and a pleading note entered her voice. "No, Alec, there's nothing wrong. Just, just l–leave me alone and I'll be fine. And please, don't tell your grandmother."

Catherine, who had been watching this interchange with an open interest untempered by guilt, since there was really no way she could avoid doing so, noted that Alec glanced uneasily at herself at this point.

"I won't if you don't want me to," he said. "But I can't just leave you alone in such a state, Sophie. Surely you can see that."

"Well, I *don't* see it," Sophie said with a slightly frantic note of bravado. "Go away." And saying that, she turned, as if to return the way she had come.

Catherine knew she ought not to interfere in something that was clearly not any business of hers, but she was moved to action not only by the woebegone expression on Sophie's face, but also by the frustrated helplessness on Alec's. The Verlains might be one of the noblest families in the land, but it struck her that they were making a sad mull of this affair. It was clear that Sophie was not so much loath to receive aid, but rather reluctant to admit a problem to any member of her husband's family. Her plea to Alec Carrock had only underlined the impression that Catherine had already received in Hookham's Library the week before, that Sophie went in considerable awe, possibly even fear, of the old duchess.

Impulsively, Catherine ran to Sophie's side. "I don't know what's wrong, and I don't want to. But it's not good for you to be walking around imitating a watering pot like this. You might fall in the lake, and then where would you be? Eaten by the carp, no doubt."

This sally, unlike Alec's attempt at humor, produced a slightly watery smile. Encouraged, Catherine took her hand and drew her down to sit beside her on one of the stone benches.

"I can see you don't want to talk, but how about coming and sitting with my dear Jane until you feel a little better? We could get you a nice cup of tea. . . ."

Sophie giggled suddenly. "Do Italians drink tea? I thought that was only the English cure for all evils. You sound just like my dearest Tilly. She used to be my governess, you know. Before I . . ." Her face crumpled again. "But there's no good thinking of that. I'll never see Tilly again. She's not good enough for me now I'm a duchess. Oh, I just wish I were dead."

Catherine looked at Alec, a question on her face. He shrugged his shoulders. Catherine accepted that he was not privy to any information on this matter, and reapplied herself to Sophie. "But doesn't a cup of tea sound nice? My Jane—she's English, you see—has been recommending it as the sovereign cure for over twenty years now. At least, that's how long she's been recommending it to me. It's probably really been a lot longer." She tugged at Sophie's hand. "Come, if you'll just walk with me. See, you're not really crying any more, and maybe Mr. Carrock will lend you his handkerchief. I'm sure it's a much more efficient one than either yours or mine is. Gentlemen's usually are." She turned to Alec. "Is it, sir?"

"What, more efficient than Sophie's? Well, it could hardly be less, could it?" he asked with a straight face, regarding the soaking scrap of lace that Catherine had removed from Sophie's hand. He produced from a pocket a large, pristine square of snowy white linen. "Here you are, my dear. You have to admit that it is at least a little less damp."

Surprisingly, Sophie essayed another little giggle. She took the proffered square and dabbed her eyes, then defiantly gave her nose a hearty blow.

"There you are," Catherine applauded. "Now, don't you feel a lot better?"

Sophie smiled. "I think a little tea would be nice. And your Jane sounds awfully nice too."

"Oh, she is," Catherine affirmed. "Just the nicest person in the world. So come along, now." She placed Sophie's hand on her arm, and gestured to Alec to do the same on the other side. Then, chattering volubly but inconsequently, she moved the little group back in the direction of the bridge and the main party.

Ten minutes later, Sophie had been ensconced snugly beside Jane inside the house, with Catherine's shawl wrapped around her shoulders and a cup of hot tea in her hand.

"It's sovereign for shocks," Jane had said comfortably,

which comment had won another tentative smile from Sophie.

"The marchesa said you would say that," she confided shyly.

"Did she?" Jane replied. "Well, it's true, and I've always said so. Caterina laughs at me, but you see she still turns to me when there's trouble." She looked up at Catherine and Alec. "Now you two run off and leave us. As you can see, the duchess and I are going to be quite happy here on our own."

Catherine twinkled at Alec. "See how she keeps me in line, Mr. Carrock. I told you she was the only reason I'm not spoilt rotten."

"That's as may be," Jane said quellingly.

Alec smiled. "Well, the results have been very good, I must say, Miss Verne. Please accept my congratulations."

Catherine, to her surprise, blushed, and accepted Alec's proffered arm without a word.

When they had returned outside, he smiled down at her. "I want to thank you," he said. "I'm very fond of Sophie. I think many people find her a silly little thing, but she's extremely good-natured and pathetically grateful for kindness."

"Which she doesn't seem to get much of," Catherine said impulsively.

Alec's smile vanished. "What do you mean?" he asked frostily.

"I don't mean to accuse you in any way," she hastened to assure him. "You seem very thoughtful of her. It's why I mention this to you. But forgive me for saying so, for of course I have not met the duke, but don't you think that that in some small way speaks for itself? And I cannot help but feel that the duchess does not feel comfortable with your grandmother, with whom she seems to spend a great deal of time. I thought it very clear that your cousin was far more afraid that your grandmother would find out about her distress than of anything else."

"My grandmother bullies everybody," he said roughly. "Sophie must learn to deal with that. I am sorry that I brought the matter up. I should not be boring you with family matters."

The change in his manner was abrupt, reminding Catherine far more of the man she had danced with at the Tyne ball than the charming companion she had flirted with today. "I'm sorry," she said, "I did not mean to meddle."

His smile was forced. "I did not accuse you of that, but it is too lovely a day and you too charming a companion to discuss such gloomy matters. Come, let us admire those daffodils we have driven so many miles to see."

It *was* still a lovely day, but somehow the delight had gone out of it for Catherine. Her agreeable companion of earlier was now silent and withdrawn, as if occupied with some other matter than herself, and while she knew she should not be so foolish as to mind it, somehow she could not help a sense of pique. After a few minutes and one turn of the lawn, she excused herself, ostensibly to return to the house.

Instead, she wandered towards the lake, brooding on her own distemper. She was not sure why she, who had always been so self-sufficient, should feel so distressed by a man's lack of interest. True, it had been wrong of her to be so forward in her opinions on his private affairs—she admitted to herself that she had been verging on impertinent—but she had never been one to cry over spilt milk or regret mistakes she had already made. Brooding, she hardly noticed where she was walking until she heard conversation.

"Ten pounds on the small green one in the very center."

"Fifteen that it's the brown-spotted one on the largest lily pad."

Startled, Catherine looked up. Six gentlemen were clustered together just in front of her, all concentrating intently on a cluster of lily pads floating at the edge of the lake. Catherine knew that propriety dictated that she turn unobtrusively and leave, for it was obvious that the gentlemen were gambling, but curiosity overcame propriety. Also, she rather thought that the marchesa would have stayed. It added a piquancy to her character to be unexpected.

So instead of turning away, she walked boldly up to the group, saying "Good afternoon, gentlemen."

Startled, they turned as one man, but remained speechless at her audacity. One gentleman, who was a number of years older and far suaver than the others, who were for the most part mere boys, recovered his aplomb first. Catherine thought she had been introduced to him at the Dowager Duchess of Tyne's ball as Sir William Meysey.

"Excuse me, ma'am," he said smoothly, "I'm sorry that you have stumbled upon our sporting activities. Do allow one of us to escort you back to the house and the rest of the party." He cast an eye around the group and chose a young gentleman of decided fashion, whose starched neckcloth and high shirt collar points made it difficult for him to turn his head. "You, Bracknell. I'm sure that Mr. Bracknell will be charmed to escort you back to the house."

"I say, Meysey," young Mr. Bracknell protested. "That's a bit stiff. I'm convinced that my frog is the winner here. You're not going to count me out on this one."

Sir William fixed him with a glare, and he wilted perceptibly before the older man.

"Well, of course," he hastened to agree. "Ladies always come first. Ma'am . . .?"

"Oh, no, gentlemen," Catherine said firmly. "You must not let me disturb you at your pursuits. Please behave as if I were not here. I will watch in complete silence and with bated breath." And so saying, she sank gracefully onto a stone bench that stood nearby, arranging her white muslin skirts gracefully around her, and allowing a slippered foot to peep out. She was pleased to notice that while the white muslin was the exemplar of purity, it still showed the line of her thigh in an intriguing manner. She had the marchesa's reputation to keep up, after all.

The gentlemen looked dubious—this was not accepted behavior as they knew it—but clearly decided that one could never tell what a foreigner, and an Italian at that, might take into her head. They turned back to their sport.

Catherine watched with a mild amount of interest, her attention focused far more on the characters of the gentlemen than on the wager in progress, which seemed to concern which frog would jump off his lily pad first. It all seemed silly, but not much different than the men she had seen in gambling dens all over Europe, who had continued to stake vast quantities of money on cards that had turned against them. Catherine had on several occasions managed to win a great deal of money from such gentlemen.

The atmosphere was in general lighthearted, the pastime of young men who had been forced by mothers or sisters to attend a function they found boring. The only exception was Sir William, whom Catherine regarded with interest from beneath lowered eyelashes. There was an intensity about his participation that reminded her of certain gentlemen she had met over the years, ones who had allowed a fever for gaming to overcome their common sense, if they had ever had any. She thought that Sir William must be nearing forty, and it spoke volumes for his interest in the wager at hand that he was willing to engage in it with these young men, most of whom were barely into their twenties. She tucked this observation away in the back of her mind. One never knew when the possession of one little fact could be a help.

Musing upon these matters, she had omitted to pay any attention to the lawn behind her until her thoughts were interrupted by what she felt she could best describe as a cry of outrage.

"Marchesa!"

She turned her head. Mr. Alec Carrock was advancing across the grass, and even at the distance of about five paces it was hard to miss the anger on his face.

She smiled inwardly; she should have known that Mr.

Carrock would not approve of the marchesa's latest activity. He seemed a most correct gentleman. She did not, however, let any indications of her thoughts cross her face, but rather rose gracefully to her feet and moved away from the gamblers. She wondered what Mr. Carrock would say if he knew that she had first entered a gambling den at the age of ten. She had been dressed as a boy, of course, but even then she had carried a small pistol unobtrusively upon her person, and upon occasion had been forced to use it.

"Marchesa," repeated Mr. Carrock more moderately, "you will remember that I had promised you a ride home. I had come to find you." It was clear from the frostiness of his tone that he wished to convey his regret that he had made any such commitment.

Catherine opted to ignore the blatant chill. "Oh, thank you," she said, and placed a hand lightly on his arm. "I must admit that I was starting to find the party tedious. Let us go now." She smiled up at him, as if she didn't see the anger on his face.

"Were you finding it tedious?" he asked. "I saw no indication back there."

"La, sir," she said lightly. "I had to find something to do."

Alec looked around, as if to check that they were alone. Since they had by this time walked some distance from the gamblers by the lake, there was nobody within hearing distance.

"May I make a humble request?" he said in a low, furious voice.

Catherine laughed, but inside, to her surprise, she found she was quaking. Why should she care what this man thought of her? she wondered with a sudden start. Was she not the same woman who had stood up to Spanish banditos at age twenty-three with a loaded pistol, and an enraged Italian colonel with a sword not so many weeks before?

"Certainly, sir," she said.

"It is of course none of my business how you care to

comport yourself, although why you should have chosen to have displayed yourself in a way that could only be interpreted as fast, I have no idea. Surely even in Italy such behavior is not condoned in a well-bred young lady."

Catherine's color rose. "I hope that I am generally considered well-bred, since my family is one of the oldest in Venice—" one side of her noted with pleasure that even in her anger she still remembered her role—"although perhaps the problem is that I am no longer young. But the matter of greatest concern to me is that you are quite right. It is none of your damned business."

"So you swear too," he said. "How admirable. But it is my damned business to this extent. You have seen fit to involve yourself with my family, and I have no wish to see my family's name smirched by such behavior."

"How dare you?" she said, her eyes flashing. "I am not 'involved' with your family. I care nothing for them."

"You have let my grandmother as good as sponsor you into London society. If that is not involvement, I don't know what is. I told my grandmother at the time that I had doubts about your background. You arrived in this town without a word of warning, nobody seems to have heard of you or your family, but because my grandmother occasionally takes a foolish start into her head, she has decided to favor you. I have no idea if you are who you say you are, but the very least you can do is behave in a manner appropriate to someone my grandmother has seen fit to ally her name with."

By main force of will, Catherine placed a rein on her own temper, for it would not help her masquerade to make a foolish, unconsidered remark.

"Your grandmother seems fully capable of taking care of herself," she said coolly. "Does she ask you to fight her battles for her?"

He whitened, and started to say something, then bit it back. She realized suddenly that she had hit a nerve.

"You are quite right," he said finally. "My grandmother

can fight her own battles. But Sophie is another matter. She is young and inexperienced, and might take your behavior as something she could emulate. You were very kind to her today. I appreciate that, but if you are to set an example such as I saw just now, I must ask you to keep away from her."

She found that the softening in his voice and manner had won her over to his point of view as his anger had not. She was used to playing her own game, and she almost never involved people who did not deserve as good as they got. She thought that the dowager duchess was far too powerful to be harmed by anything she could do, and had felt no qualms at using the woman in her schemes. But when she had acted to befriend Sophie, she had done so impulsively, not considering any consequence; certainly she had not meant to harm the child in the way that Alec Carrock was accusing her.

She laid a gentle hand on his arm and smiled up at him. "Was what I did really so reprehensible?" she asked. Her eyes twinkled and a dimple appeared in her cheek. "I can think of much worse, you know."

He chuckled. "Can you? Yes, I suppose you could. Just don't communicate them to Sophie, if you please."

"Will you still drive me home?" she asked. "Or am I to be abandoned here as punishment?"

"Good Lord, no. I would never do that," he said, obviously shocked.

"Did you bring your greys?" she asked. "I saw you driving them in the park the other day. They are beautiful creatures. I longed to drive them myself."

"Could you do so?" he asked, intrigued despite himself. "They are mettlesome creatures, not suited for a woman."

"I don't know," she said honestly. "But I have driven a few spirited teams in my time." She thought she would not mention she had most often done so while employed as a groom when she was seventeen.

He laughed. "Shall I let you try them? When we get out on an open stretch of road?"

"I would be delighted," she said. Her eyes twinkled. "Although something tells me that that is perhaps no more acceptable behaviour than what you were just raking me over the coals for."

"Oh no," he said seriously. "Not in an open carriage. My tiger will be with us. It is perfectly proper. I would never have invited you else. You don't have to worry. . . ."

He realized she was laughing.

"Ah, Marchesa, you are a complete hand. Shall we call it even." He held out a hand. "Truce?"

She grasped it. His long, strong fingers closed around hers, and she wondered at the thrill that ran up her spine.

"Truce," she said, returning the handshake.

5

Alexander Carrock's greys were a justly famous pair. They had been bred for him by his cousin the Duke of Tyne, and while Anthony Verlain's intelligence was not frequently considered to be of the highest order, there could be no question that the man was an expert when it came to horseflesh. Alec's pair were full brothers, a year apart in age, and so like that few could tell any difference between them. They were seven and eight years old now, and in the prime of life. Alec had won several well-publicized races with them, but they also possessed a sweetness that matched their speed.

They were his pride and joy, so he was extremely pleased when the marchesa uttered a low sound of admiration when his tiger brought them around.

"They're lovely," she said. "I didn't have a true chance to see their best points when you trotted by in the park the other day."

Alec smiled. "If you're trying to win me over, you've found much the best way, ma'am."

"Oh, no. I mean it entirely. *Will* you really let me drive them? Just for a few moments, perhaps. I promise I won't let them run away, or drop them so they stumble."

Alec considered the matter. He seldom let anybody drive his greys, and certainly had never let a woman. But this woman, with her firm, clear gaze, her quiet air of competence, was in some way different. He thought somehow that he could trust her with them. "All right," he said.

"When we get out of the lane, but before we encounter the London traffic, I don't see why not."

He wondered immediately if he were mad, but when he saw her green eyes sparkle with pleasure, all such considerations left him.

With considerable expertise, he helped her up into the phaeton, which stood some distance above shoulder height. Leaving the little tiger Jem to hold the horses' heads, he ran round and swung himself up. Expertly picking up the reins of the fretting horses, he called to Jem to let the horses go, and allowed them lead off at a canter as Jem scrambled up behind. In a moment they were down the drive and Alec was expertly feathering the corner around the stone gateposts and out into the lane. He couldn't resist looking around at the Marchesa to gauge her reaction.

"Showoff," she said, with a smile that set a dimple flickering in her little three-cornered face.

He grinned. "Well . . . yes. But you had seemed interested."

"You're good," she added, with a cool, analytical detachment.

"Thank you" was all he said, but he found that her words had set his pulses to thundering. Somehow this restrained praise meant more to him than the far more lavish compliments that most women would have handed out, women who were more concerned with impressing him than telling the truth.

The horses were fresh, for he had driven them easily on the way out, and they had rested over two hours. They fretted at the bit, and this gave him the excuse to focus most of his attention on them. But as he turned them out of the narrow lane onto the main London road, he looked again at the marchesa.

"I will let you drive them, as I promised, but I'd like to take a bit of the edge off them first. Do you mind if I spring them for a few minutes?"

"I'd love it," she said.

The road in front of them was empty for a stretch of a few miles. "Hang on," he said, and gave the greys their head.

They seized it eagerly, and the road flew away beneath their feet. Catherine gasped with pleasure as the wind hit her in the face, threatening to tear off the frivolous bergere straw hat. She reached up with one hand to grasp it, still hanging onto the phaeton with the other, but had nearly lost the unequal struggle with the hat when Alec reined the greys in to a walk.

"Did you like that?" he asked.

"I loved it," she cried. "It's been far too long since I've had a chance to go that fast." She was remembering the wild gallops she had taken the year they had lived in Spain; they had been mewed up in cities since then.

"Did you get that many chances to drive in Venice?" he asked, curiosity evident in his voice.

Damn, Catherine thought. She had let her enthusiasm tempt her into indiscretions. Luckily, there was an easy way out of this one.

"Oh, everybody leaves Venice during the summer and goes out to their country homes. It gets far too hot and stuffy to stay in the city. If you could just smell it. And of course, we take gondolas over to the Lido and ride there during the winter. I assure you, sir, I do know my way around horses."

"I wasn't meaning to doubt that," he said quickly. "You can take them now, if you like. I think they've had a chance to breathe."

"They were barely winded," Catherine said admiringly. "I'm impressed with their stamina."

She held out her hands for the reins, and Alec passed them and the whip over. She found she had been waiting for the light touch of his hands on hers.

"Keep a light hold on their mouths, and just let them trot along easily," Alec said. "They should be pretty obedient now."

She followed his directions, and they trotted in high style up the road, Catherine exhilarated at the feel of a pair of really sweet goers, Alec sneaking an occasional glance at her rapt face.

Her enthusiasm was enchanting, he thought, her changeable, multi-faceted personality intriguing. Who would have guessed that this was the same sophisticate who had all of London at her feet? And who would have thought she would be the kind of woman to show such kindness and tact with Sophie? His experience of women had taught him that their relationships with each other were frequently more on the order of a catfight. Even his mother had been unable to spend more than a day or two at a time with his grandmother without some squabble breaking out, although the two had always presented a united front to any who had attempted to gainsay either. He wondered if Caterina's kindness was genuine, or whether, as was so often true, it was a facade that she put up merely to benefit herself.

"I think I'd better take them back now," he said, rousing himself from his thoughts. "I can see a few other carriages up ahead, and we'll be reaching London soon."

Catherine handed over the reins, and smiled up at him, her face glowing with fresh air and enthusiasm.

"Thank you," she said sincerely. "I enjoyed that. I appreciate your trust."

"I enjoyed seeing you do it. You're a fine driver. Did you learn from your father?"

"Yes," said Catherine. That, at least, was the truth. She found she had no desire to elaborate with lies. Deception had always been a game before, but then she had never before found herself coming to like and admire anyone she set out to deceive.

The rest of the journey into London was accomplished in relative silence. Only at the end, when they had drawn up in front of Catherine's house in Portman Square, did either say anything but the most basic trivialities.

But when he had handed Catherine down from the carriage, Alec stopped her for a moment. "I am sorry I was angry earlier. I honestly doubt very much that you would be the bad influence on Sophie that I accused you of being." He smiled. "Perhaps what she needs is a little of your self-confidence, even if it does occasionally lead you into what I consider inappropriate behaviour. I strongly suggest that your friendship might be just what she needs. Could I ask that of you? That you be her friend?"

The glow Catherine felt should have been the result of a well-laid plan arriving at fruition. She had come to London to infiltrate society, to impress the best families with her story, to convince them that she and her father were the Italian nobility they called themselves. She was accomplishing just that. But instead she knew that what she was feeling was joy that Alec Carrock admired and trusted her. And mixed with that feeling was more than a touch of shame—because if he knew how little of what she had told him was the truth, he would never have offered such a trust.

The note was inscribed on cream-colored vellum, and borne by a footman in the resplendent Tyne livery. On the outside it said formally "The Marchesa di Carabas" in beautiful copperplate script. The inside was considerably less proper.

"My dear Caterina," it said in a hurried handwriting. "Oh, I do so Hope you don't mind if I call you that. I truly Enjoyed the time I spent with you and your Delightful Miss Verne, and am so hoping that both of you will be kind enough to come and call on me at Tyne House very soon. Yours, Sophie, Duchess of Tyne."

The "Sophie" was as hurried and as natural as the text of the letter. The "Duchess of Tyne" appeared to have been inscribed very much as an afterthought, in the same careful copperplate as the outside.

Catherine, receiving this note just two mornings after

the *al fresco* party at Lady Harrington's, took it upstairs to Jane, who had very unusually sent word that she would not be coming down to breakfast. She found Jane still in bed, sneezing rather dolefully into a large handkerchief.

"I think I have a cold," she explained in answer to Catherine's inquiring look.

"You unquestionably have a cold," said Catherine. "You poor thing, you look absolutely miserable. What a pity that it should be now, too. I've just received an invitation for us to pay a morning call—at least I presume that is what it's an invitation for, she's really not very specific—on that little Sophie child. But of course, since you're obviously not well, we'll have to put it off for a while."

"Oh no," Jane said, her tones still firm despite the blockage in her nose. She was not the mastermind behind the Browns' schemes, but she had never hesitated to advise Catherine when she thought it was necessary. "I hope you're not contemplating passing up the best chance you've had yet to become an intimate of London society. What would your father say? And also—and if you ask me this is far more important—I think the little Duchess badly needs a friend. She didn't say much to me, but I rather got the impression that nobody ever has a kind word for her except your Mr. Carrock. Certainly that overbearing grandmother-in-law of hers doesn't. And her husband has been out of town for nearly a month, she said. Shocking behavior in a man who has barely been married a year, if you ask me."

Catherine grinned. "I gather you feel strongly on the subject, Janey. If you're sure that you don't feel too poorly to be left alone, perhaps I should go this morning."

"I feel perfectly fine, if a little stuffy around the nose. At least I will if I'm left alone in bed and not required to think. I have quite a stack of books from Hookham's which I have not had a chance to look at yet, and if I get tired of that I thought I would do the hem on your riding habit. Just because you have not as yet had any need for it does not mean that you might not be invited to take a ride somewhere."

Catherine was unsure as to the wisdom of this latter activity, but agreed to leave after extracting a promise from Jane that she would not embark on any sewing unless she truly felt like it.

When Catherine's hansom pulled up at Tyne House as early as convention permitted, the front door immediately opened and a footman descended to open the door of the carriage. He waited with stoic calm on his face for her to pay off the driver, then escorted her up the steps with due solemnity. The door was flung open by another footman, and the butler advanced to greet her.

"The Marchesa di Carabas, I believe," he said.

"Well," said Catherine, impressed and irrepressible. "That's very good, I must say. And I've only been here once. I wish that our Italian servants had half your memory."

"Thank you, M'lady," said Brothers with no lightening of his austerity. "Her Grace is in the Yellow Parlor. I believe she was expecting you to call." He did not add, since this was not part of his function, that the little duchess had been in a dither of anticipation all morning, petrified that her overtures of friendship would not be responded to positively. He had finally had to suggest in his most overbearing fashion that she sit quietly with a tea tray. Brothers was glad that the Marchesa had seen fit to respond so promptly to the invitation; many ladies would not have done so, he reflected.

Preceding her down the echoing marble hall, he flung open the door and announced portentiously, "The Marchesa di Carabas."

There was a scuffle from within, and Catherine, passing into the room, was privileged to see Sophie jump up and nearly overset the tea tray in the process. A minute pug, thus rudely dispossessed from her lap, leaped agilely to the floor and signified its disapproval by barking vociferously.

With a smile on her face, Catherine advanced into the room, but the pug was far nimbler than either she or Sophie. Reaching Catherine's feet, it proceeded to circle them, indulging in amazing leaps that came nearly to her knees. Charmed, Catherine knelt down to talk to it, and it promptly leaped up to lick her face. Its velocity however, was perhaps greater than it realized, for it collided with Catherine's nose rather suddenly.

Catherine laughed and, setting a firm hand on it, gathered it into her arms. It wiggled there, but this seemed to be merely from an excess of energy than any disinclination to stay. For the first time Catherine was able to take a close look. It was a compact bundle of muscle covered by fawn-and-black velvet, with a funny, squinched-up nose and a most endearing pink tongue.

"Why, this has to be a puppy!" she exclaimed. "They aren't really this small, are they? What's its name?"

Sophie's eyes lit up. "Oh, do you like him? His name's Valancourt—out of *Mysteries of Udolpho*, you know—and he was just four months old yesterday. I'm so glad you like him."

Valancourt, hearing his name, wriggled from Catherine's arms and ran across the room to Sophie, who picked him up and held him to her chest. "Oh, Val," she said, "you have an admirer."

She bent her head and dropped a kiss on the tip of the puppy's retroussé nose, then raised her face in consternation. "Oh, dear, but I'm being a terrible hostess. The dowager would be shocked at me. Please do sit down, my dear Marchesa. And can I offer you some tea? I will ring for a fresh pot. Have you eaten? I had a small nuncheon just recently, but we could offer you some sandwiches, I am sure." Throughout this scattered speech, she was darting to and fro, first towards the sofa, then towards the bell pull, then back towards the sofa, and finally standing in distress in the middle of the room.

Catherine laughed. "Do not disturb yourself so much,

my dear. A fresh pot of tea would be very pleasant, but I have already eaten. Ring for the tea, but then do come and sit with me." Moving to the sofa, she sat down on one end. Valancourt, who seemed unable to stay still for more than a moment, jumped from Sophie's distracted arms and, bouncing across the room, hopped up beside her. "And I thought that you were going to call me Caterina," Catherine added. "May I call you Sophie?"

"Oh, yes," Sophie said, coming to sit beside her. "I would like that. It gets very lonely sometimes, for my family is not in town this year. My sister Eugenia, who is the next oldest after me, is over two years younger than me, and won't be sixteen for another few months. I think my mother would have liked to present her this year, for now that I have married so well I will be able to escort Genie around and be able to get her invitations to all the best parties, but even Mama realizes that fifteen is too young to be presented. But they can't afford to come up for the Season unless one of us is to be presented, for there are six of us girls, you know. Mama was so glad that I made such an eligible match. She was hoping and hoping when Tony started to pay such attention to me, but she really couldn't believe it, for the Duke of Tyne. . . . Well, you must see, it seemed very unlikely when there are six of us, and we have so little money, and Papa is only a baronet, and not even an important one."

She paused for breath, and at that moment a footman came in with a new teatray. When all had been settled, and the footman had left again, Catherine reopened the conversation.

"I gather the duke is not in town right now?"

"Oh, no. Tony doesn't really like the Season; he only comes at all because the dowager tells him he should. Of course, he would keep the house open anyway because the dowager would want to be here, but she feels that he should be in residence himself. She is very upset right now because he went to Newmarket for the races. He has several horses running there, I believe. Tony is always doing something with horses. He has quite a few racehorses, and when there's not racing he's hunting, so he keeps hunters as well, mostly at his hunting box in the Shires, so that I have never seen them." Her pretty, expressive little face showed some distress.

"I hoped maybe he would take me there with him, although Grandmama says that gentlemen never take their *wives* to hunting boxes. But Tony's not that type. At least, I don't think he is. I think it's more because I was frightened of his horses at first. I do like horses when I get to know them. I had a lovely, sweet old gelding that Genie and I shared, but big horses frighten me, and Tony's—the ones I've seen, I mean—are all especially big. I believe he gets them from Ireland.

"He has dogs, too, so that in the winter, on the days when he can't hunt, he goes out shooting. But they're such big rough dogs, and they track all over the house with their muddy paws and get fur on my dresses. That's why I got Valancourt, because Tony's dogs were all so big and I couldn't really feel fond of them. I thought maybe that Tony would like it that I had a dog, too, but he just laughed at poor little Valancourt and said he was silly." The indignation on Sophie's face was so intense that Catherine had to forcibly control her laughter.

"Alec is the only person who likes poor Val," Sophie continued. "The dowager says he's nuisance, and that he yaps and gives her a headache. Which he does, of course. Yap, I mean. I don't know about the headache."

Her hand went to her mouth in a gesture of distress. "Oh, dear, I shouldn't have said that. About the headache, I mean. Of course if the dowager says he gives her one then he must. But she's not going to make me give up my little Val." She reached over and drew Valancourt into her lap protectively. He snuggled up against her hand in a touching gesture of affection. Sophie looked down at him and smiled, and her pretty face, which frequently in repose had a pathetic look that reminded Catherine of a mourning Renaissance madonna, sparkled. Then she looked conscience-stricken. "But I can't believe how I'm babbling on. I should be letting you talk. I'm terribly sorry. I'm not usually so rude."

"That's quite all right," Catherine said, laughing. "I can see that you have definitely decided that we will be friends. I'm delighted, for it is very lonely for me here all alone in London, you know. I miss my father."

"Oh," said Sophie. Her face showed her concern. "How terrible you must feel. I miss Genie and my sisters awfully sometimes. I'm not used to being as alone as I have been. . . ." She broke off in consternation, and despite Catherine's encouraging silence refused to complete her sentence. "Did you tell Alec that your father was coming to join you later in the Season? He said something of the sort to me."

Catherine felt a strange, unexplainable glow that Alec had indeed thought enough of her to talk of her to Sophie. "Yes," she said, "he had to complete some business affairs in Venezia, Venice I mean, before we left, and I was too impatient. I was afraid that I would miss most of the London season. So I came on ahead. But he should be here by June at the latest, I think."

"Oh, I'm glad to hear that," Sophie said. "I am hoping that once we go to Northumberland for the summer, that Grandmother will allow me to invite Genie to visit me. Then I will have that to look forward to. It was very hard last year, especially in the autumn, for Tony was in the Shires hunting, and I was up in Northumberland with Grandmother at Tyne. I think if Alec had not been there I would have gone quite mad. It was better during the winter, when Tony came up to Tyne, and Christmas was even quite fun at times, at least it would have been if Tony—" She broke off suddenly, obviously unwilling to express this last thought.

Catherine was fascinated by these unwitting revelations

of the intricate relations among the Tyne family, especially, though she would have liked to deny it, by Alec's role.

"Mr. Carrock is your husband's cousin?" she asked. "But through the female side, I collect."

"Alec's mother was Tony's father's sister. She married Mr. John Carrock, who was an extremely eminent gentleman in Cumberland. But he died very young, when Alec was barely eight, I gather, and his mother came back to live with the dowager duchess." Sophie gave a shiver, as if the thought disturbed her, but did not elucidate her disquietude. "Well," she said brightly, "I keep talking on about me. I want to hear all about you. Are you enjoying London? Is it as amusing as you thought it would be?"

"Oh, it's lovely," Catherine said automatically, while her thoughts remained obstinately fixed on Alec Carrock. It must have been a strange childhood for him, she thought, being brought up by two women, especially if one were the Dowager Duchess of Tyne. Almost as strange as her own wandering life with only her father, although Alec, of course, had the stability of a home. But then she had also had Jane, something that she would never underrate.

"I find the English people so charming and kind to me," she said in answer to Sophie's question, and would have continued if the noise of someone else arriving had not sounded in the hall right then.

"I wonder who that is," Sophie said. "Grandmother is out until dinner. That's why I hoped you would come today."

The door opened, and Brothers appeared to announce, "Sir William Meysey."

Sophie murmured something under her breath, which sounded remarkably like "Oh, dear" to Catherine, but she stood up and shook her skirts out, then advanced to meet Sir William with aplomb.

"Sir William, how good of you to call."

"My dear Duchess, I had to. To make sure that—"

"Oh, Sir William," Sophie interrupted, with what seemed like haste, "have you met my dearest new friend, the Marchesa di Carabas?" She turned so that Catherine would be included in the conversation.

Catherine thought she saw a shade of annoyance cross Sir William's face when he realized there was someone in the room, but he recovered quickly.

"Marchesa, I'm charmed to meet you under more congenial circumstances."

Catherine nearly blushed at this reference to the gambling episode. She didn't mind what Sir William thought of her, but Alec Carrock's good opinion had apparently become important. She wondered why it should be. "I think a drawing room is frequently more congenial than a windswept lawn," was all she said, however.

"Well, let us all sit down," Sophie said. "I won't ask Sir William if he wants tea; I know he can't abide the stuff. But perhaps some sherry?"

"Oh, no, my dear duchess, do not put yourself out. I had not really intended to stay for long. I would not want to interrupt your comfortable coze with your friend." There was an ironic edge to his tone that implied he meant exactly the opposite.

The conversation that followed was desultory, with Sophie bearing the chief part in it. Catherine became possessed of the distinct impression that Sir William was hoping she would take her departure, leaving him alone with Sophie. Her curiosity aroused, she determined to outstay him. Possibly she might have succeeded, for Sir William was getting clearly more irritable by the minute, if sounds of conversation in the hall had not heralded another visitor.

"No need to get stuffy on me, Brothers. I don't need to be announced," said a voice clearly, and Alec Carrock entered the room most unceremoniously, a breezy smile on his face.

6

As APPEARED TO be its habit whenever anyone new arrived—although now that Catherine thought of it, the animal had been conspicuously silent at Sir William's arrival—the pug flung itself from the sofa with a flurry of barks. Bouncing across the room it circled Alec's boots with enthusiasm, and finally attempted to scale the summit.

With an ease obviously due to long association, Alec reached down and held it off with one hand.

"Sophie, can you call off your vicious hound?" he asked, a grin on his face.

"Oh, dear," Sophie said, then realized suddenly that he was joking. "Here, Valancourt," she called, patting the sofa beside her, and the little dog regretfully left Mr. Carrock's boots to resume its place beside her.

Alec scanned the room. "Quite a little soirée here today, Sophie. I suppose that is what Brothers was trying to tell me. Marchesa, your devoted. Sir William." His tone made it abundantly clear that he did not number Sir William among his more favored acquaintances, at least not when the man was to be found in Sophie's drawing room.

"I came to visit Grandmama, Sophie," he said. "I haven't seen her since the day of Lady Harrington's party, and I'm afraid I neglected her shamefully there."

"She went out to Richmond to see Cousin Lavinia and Cousin Gertrude," Sophie said. "I don't think she was planning to be back until dinner. But she did want me to go with her to the Countess of Sudbury's musicale tonight, so I don't think she'll be too late."

"Well, as long as you tell her I came by. I'm not cooling my heels here until then."

"Oh, I'm sure Grandmother wouldn't expect that," Sophie said.

"I'm sure she does expect it, but it can't be helped. I have better things to do." He regarded Sir William with a jaundiced eye. "Meysey, were you on your way somewhere? May I take you up?"

"No, no, Carrock, you mustn't trouble yourself," said Sir William blandly.

"It would be no trouble at all," Alec persisted.

Catherine sighed inwardly. It was obvious that Alec was as suspicious of the implications of Sir William's presence as she was herself, but she felt he was handling the situation badly. The man was clearly well-meaning, but he needed education in duplicity.

Smiling sweetly, she stood up, and both men politely rose with her. "Perhaps you could take me up, Mr. Carrock. I must be getting back to Portman Square, since I left my dear Jane with a cold."

Alec's demeanor was not a model of complaisance, but he submitted with grace. "I would be charmed, Marchesa," he said, rising and bowing.

"Thank you," said Catherine, observing with interest out of the corner of her eye the look of smug satisfaction on Sir William's face. If Alec's scowl indicated anything, then he had apparently noticed as well.

Alec had brought his phaeton, and the short drive to Portman Square was accomplished with light conversation on Catherine's part and silence on his. Catherine might have been piqued by his apparent lack of interest in herself, but she thought he was brooding about Sophie's problems, and so forgave him. Those problems were on her mind, too, but she concealed her thoughts with a flow of light gossip until the right moment came. Only when they had actually arrived in front of the house Catherine had rented for the season did she cease to chatter.

Alec had dismounted from his side of the curricle, the tiger having already run to the horses' heads, and was reaching up his hand to help Catherine climb down. She rested one tan-gloved hand in his and jumped neatly down, landing beside him and resting for a moment within the circle of his arm.

When he would have moved away, she placed a hand detainingly on his shoulder. "Wait a minute," she said. "You're going about this all wrong, you know."

He frowned. "What are you talking about?" he asked a little too sharply.

"You're being much too obvious. The duchess may be young, but she's not a child. And you're annoying Sir William."

"I meant to," he said crisply.

"You'll not gain anything except trouble that way," she pointed out patiently. "You're showing your hand far too soon."

His eyes showed his interest. "So you too think there's something wrong there?"

"Perhaps. Do you know Sir William well?"

"Somewhat," he said. "He's not a close acquaintance, if that's what you mean. We have different interests."

"You're not a gambler?" she said bluntly.

He was wearing an oddly arrested expression. "Exactly, ma'am."

"Does your cousin know him well?"

"Sophie, you mean?"

She nodded.

"Until a few weeks ago, I would have thought not. But of late he seems to have been hanging around her far too much. Damn, I wish Tony would come back to town and take care of his own wife. I've thought of talking to Grandmother about the matter, but. . . ." His voice trailed off, as if he had suddenly realized that he was being indiscreet.

Catherine finished the sentence for him. "But your grandmother would just make matters worse."

He flushed slightly, a faint line of rose that highlighted the brown skin over his prominent cheekbones. "Yes," he said finally. "You were absolutely right at Richmond, of course. Grandmother is a wonderful woman, please don't mistake me, but she can be domineering with Sophie sometimes."

"And with you?" she asked.

"I love her," he said defensively.

"I wasn't questioning that. I love my father, but he always has to pipe the tune. One learns to live with it, if one has grown up with it and loves the other person. But your cousin doesn't have either of those advantages, you know."

"No," he said. "I do know that."

"Forgive me," Catherine said, "but I can't help wondering about her relationship with the duke. I realize that arranged marriages are common—certainly we have our share of them in Italy—but the duchess is an appealing child. Surely the duke could find it in himself to make her a little happier."

"Is she so unhappy, do you think?" Alec asked softly. "I know Grandmama bullies her, but when I ask her about it she won't tell me. And she does seem to have her amusements, to have found her feet in town. I thought perhaps if you were to be a friend to her . . . ?"

"I think she's quite desperately lonely," Catherine said bluntly. "And I think she needs a husband, not a friend, although I am certainly happy to be that to her, if she is willing. We were having a delightful time until Sir William arrived."

"I'll write to Tony," he said. "I don't know. I'm no expert in these affairs. But at the very least the man should keep an eye on his own wife. I wouldn't trust Meysey further than I could throw a pikestaff." He grinned. "Not that I've ever thrown one, of course. So that's not very far at all."

"Quite," said Catherine. She realized suddenly how close she had been standing to Alec throughout this exchange, and stepped backward. "I hope you don't consider me unduly interfering."

"You are a ridiculously interfering female," he said. "I told you that at Richmond. But I have to admit that every word you've said so far has been of extraordinary good sense. And that's something I think my family holds in remarkably short supply."

He moved towards her, closing the distance she had just created. Taking her gloved hand, he turned it over to expose the wrist where the glove met the sleeve, and brought it lightly to his lips. "Thank you, Marchesa, for your concern. I wish you a good day."

He bowed and, signaling to his tiger that he was ready to leave, climbed back onto the seat of his phaeton.

Catherine mounted the steps of the Portman Square house, but, ignoring the butler who had swung the door open, stood watching him out of sight, and wondering why she imagined she could still feel the imprint of his lips upon her wrist.

The notes were written on the same paper—creamy vellum with the crest of the Dukes of Tyne unobtrusively heading the page—and delivered at the same time by the same liveried footman, but the difference in tone was great.

"The Dowager Duchess of Tyne requests the honour of the presence of Caterina, Marchesa di Carabas and Miss Jane Verne at an informal dinner on the fourth day of May," said the first missive.

The second was in a slightly less formal style. "Dearest Caterina, please do say that you and Miss Verne will come to Grandmother's dinner. I do not know how I will get through it without the comfort of your presence. Tony has returned to London."

Catherine eyed this note, especially the last sentence, with interest. She had learnt over the preceding weeks that Sophie tended towards an inconsequential style, both when speaking and when writing, but she tended to believe that the final sentence in this missive was not a non sequitur. She had noticed that the young duchess seemed torn between an unspoken anger at her husband for leaving her alone with the dowager, and an apparent fear of his return.

So the errant duke had returned, had he? She wondered if it had been Mr. Carrock's letter that had done the job. She could not find it in herself to blame the man for wishing to escape his grandmother's sphere of influence, but she thought that he should not have abandoned his wife to her, either. Well, she would definitely have to attend the dinner, if just to discover what kind of a man Anthony Verlain, Third Duke of Tyne, was. It had been very hard to make much sense at all out of Sophie's frank but disjointed comments, and Mr. Carrock had been, as he often seemed to be on such subjects, reticent. With a faint crease of thought in her forehead, Catherine refolded the letters and betook herself to talk to Jane.

The Duke of Tyne turned out to be a man of some five-and-twenty years, tall, broad-shouldered, with plainly trimmed blond hair and a placid, good-humored face. He made little attempt in his dress to conform to the dictates of fashion, clearly preferring instead to affect a comfortable style, with coats he could presumably shrug into himself, and a simply tied neckcloth. When Catherine entered the drawing room of Tyne House he was sitting rather stiffly in a straight-backed, spindly gilt chair, although there would have been room beside Sophie on the sofa. Beneath the chair lay a golden and white cocker spaniel.

It was immediately obvious to Catherine that the spaniel had been the cause of some dissension, for the dowager duchess was still holding forth on the subject.

"Totally unsuitable to a gentleman's establishment," she said roundly. "My dear husband was extremely fond of the occasional shooting expedition, but the dogs returned to the kennels when the day was done. And they certainly were not brought to town, where there could be no possible need for a gun dog. I can't imagine—"

She realized suddenly that Brothers had opened the door for Catherine and Jane, and broke off suddenly.

"My dear Marchesa," she said graciously, "how kind of you to come. And Miss Verne. I want you to meet my grandson, the Duke of Tyne."

The duke rose promptly, as did Mr. Carrock, who had been sitting off to one side, apparently observing the proceedings in silence. Several minutes later, an elderly gentleman who was introduced as Sir Roderick Hastings and who was clearly an old friend of the dowager's, arrived with his callow grandson, whom Catherine deduced was in town for the first time, and completed the party. The dowager shortly after ordained that they would go down to dinner.

The spaniel jumped up in the subsequent flurry of movement, but Catherine noticed that a look from the duke and a stern "No, Honey," were enough to cause her to retreat sadly to the chair once again. Whatever other character flaws the duke might have, she ruminated, he did train his dogs.

Dinner was simple, a matter of two courses with only half-a-dozen removes at each, and the group small enough that conversation was general. Catherine had plenty of time to watch the duke—or Tony, as she was already irreverently calling him in her mind—and Sophie. She noticed that, while neither spoke to the other, Tony's eyes frequently rested on his wife when he thought nobody was watching. She found that interesting, and made a pretext after dinner to sit down next to him.

She tried several topics on him, all to little avail. The duke was polite, but his conversation seemed limited.

"I hear from the duchess that you are quite a sportsman," she said finally. "I find I miss my horses and the gallops on the Lido now that I am in London. You have no place like that here in London, I think, for in Hyde Park I am told that ladies must walk or trot demurely."

Tony made a wry face and answered with surprising animation. "Men too, I'm afraid, ma'am. I try to avoid it whenever possible."

"But surely you take the duchess," Catherine hinted.

"She's not too keen on horses, ma'am. I tried to find a horse for her at Tyne, but she told me she'd rather not. Pity. I would have liked to be able to ride with her. I'm not much of a fellow for dances and such. Fact of the matter is, don't think I'd even come up to London if m'grandmother didn't insist. Says it's the Duke's duty to do so. Now she says I should do it for Sophie's sake at least, even if I don't care for my grandmama's feelings." He reddened. "Not that I don't care for her. That's just her way of talking. Likes to say things like that." In an apparent attempt to cover his embarrassment, he reached down to fondle the spaniel's ears, relapsing into silence.

Catherine tried several other topics, but eventually gave up the fight. The duke was unfailingly polite, but seemed unwilling, or perhaps unable, to converse on topics outside the world of sports. They had made a brief foray into foxhunting, but since that was a topic Catherine knew nothing of, although she had had some experience coursing for hares with greyhounds in Portugal, she was unable to contribute much to the topic.

Several things seemed clear to her, however. The duke seemed a gentle, kind-hearted man, despite his lack of intellect or interest in matters outside of sports. And Catherine rather suspected, judging both from the way he looked at Sophie, and from the warm note that entered his voice when he spoke of her, that he held a genuine regard for his wife.

Jane, when the subject was broached to her later that evening, after their return to Portman Square, concurred. "It's a pity that the duchess seems to have gotten it into her head that he doesn't," she said bluntly. "I can't think why."

"No," said Catherine meditatively. She was stretched out across her bed, resting her chin on her hands. "It could be any number of reasons, really. Sophie's a sweet little thing, but not exactly needle-witted, I fear. I shouldn't think the dowager helps matters. That at least seems obvious. I fear, too, that if someone doesn't help Sophie out of this tangle, she's going to do something really idiotic. Mr. Carrock is trying, I will admit, but he has not the instinct for intrigue. I wish I knew what this Sir William is to her."

Jane looked at her suspiciously. "Catherine, are you going to interfere where you have no right to again?"

Catherine rolled over and looked up at Jane, her green eyes two limpid pools of innocence. "I don't know. Why?"

"Because I'm remembering that unfortunate family in Bayonne, the ones you ended up stealing a mule for. I have enough problems on my plate with the pranks your father plays, without having you getting started too."

"I won't do anything that could get us in trouble," Catherine promised. "At least I don't think I will."

Jane eyed her direfully. "Well, just remember what you're here for. You're supposed to be impressing the *ton*, not indulging in escapades."

Catherine sighed. "I do remember, Jane. I do. All the time. Sometimes I wish so much that I didn't. Will there ever be a time when all this pretense is over? I get so tired sometimes, Jane."

Jane remained silent a few moments, considering what she should say. "Not as long as you remain at your father's side, my dear," she said bluntly. "And I know you too well to believe that you'd ever leave him."

"No," said Catherine. "It's been him and you and me too long. I suppose it will be us against the world for a long time yet." But her eyes were bleak.

She lay there a long time, until Jane longed to ask her what she was thinking of, but didn't dare. Eventually, she left the room silently, but late in the night she woke to hear the sound of Catherine's footsteps, pacing up and down the room.

In the morning, although she was a little heavy-eyed, Catherine was her normal ebullient self, exuberantly planning what she should wear to Almack's that evening, and sorting through the huge pile of invitations that was, as usual, placed beside her plate at breakfast. The Marchesa di Carabas had become a wild success in London society as soon as it became clear that both the dowager duchess and the Duchess of Tyne numbered her among their friends. She was often to be seen strolling with the duchess in Hyde Park, and of course word had soon spread of the honour of an invitation to a tiny—almost family, in fact—dinner, the previous night. And then there was her exotic beauty, her charm, and her father's rumored fortune. The amount of the last was not known with any certainty, but while she might live in an area of town and in a style that was not of the highest, that could be excused because she was a foreigner, and her jewels and clothes were always Parisian and obviously fabulously expensive. In all, it was not surprising that she did not lack for male admirers.

After a while, Jane left on an errand to the Pantheon Bazaar. "For I saw some beautiful amber ribbon and matching feathers there, my dear, and I thought you could retrim one of your hats to go with the new walking dress I'm making for you. I didn't expect you'd need so many walking dresses, but since you've taken to walking with the Duchess so many days now, you really must have some more. You've worn the green one three times, and that won't do. You're just going to have to turn down any invitations you receive to go walking until we're finished."

"I suppose you're right," said Catherine. "I'll help you with the sewing later today. Do you need any money?"

"No, for thank heavens everything there is quite ridiculously cheap."

She left, and Catherine was still sitting at the table, absently sipping coffee and reading invitations, when Sophie was announced.

"Oh, Caterina," she said without preamble, as was her wont. "I'm not too early, am I? I just had to come and talk, for really things are just too dismal at Tyne House. I really had convinced myself that life would be better once Tony came back, but I can't imagine now why I thought so. He brought that dog of his, and it has made Grandmother quite livid, so that now she is saying that she doesn't think any dog belongs in a house. I am quite petrified that she will insist I give up

Valancourt, and I don't think I could stand that. He's my only friend."

"But now that your husband is home, you really shouldn't let the dowager bully you," Catherine essayed tentatively, testing the waters. "It is his house, after all."

"Oh, no, I don't dare let him know of this, for I know he despises little Val."

"But even if he doesn't like your dog—and you know, some men, especially ones who have hunting dogs themselves, are not fond of small dogs; my father is not, for instance—he will protect you because you are his wife."

Sophie's chin wobbled, and she looked down at her clasped hands for a long minute. A tear escaped and ran down her cheek. "I don't think Tony cares whether I am his wife or not," she said finally. "I try to be conformable, as Mama told me I should be, and not to fret him with my presence, but it is very hard. It was better when we were alone together at Tyne for a month in the summer after we were married last year. I thought then that perhaps we would come to like each other. I wanted to go with him to his hunting box in the Shires when he went there in the autumn. I don't know what I would have done, for I don't hunt, you know, but I thought it would be nice in the evenings, when Tony came back from hunting. But when I mentioned it to Grandmother, she told me that I was being hopelessly b–b–b–bourgeoise . . ." Her pretty little face crumpled, but with an effort she controlled herself. "Well, how was I to know?" she demanded indignantly. "*My* family never had a hunting box in the Shires. But apparently gentlemen don't expect to take their wives."

"So did you ever mention it to the duke?" Catherine asked.

"No," said Sophie. "Grandmother said I would only embarrass both him and myself if I asked."

"Oh," said Catherine, struck into silence by what could only be interpreted as a piece of malevolent meddling. She believed that the convivial parties at gentlemen's hunting boxes in the Shires were more likely to be graced by high-flyers than otherwise, but one short evening with Anthony Verlain had been enough to convince her that he wouldn't know Covent Garden ware if one jumped out of a hedge and mooed at him. Whatever anybody else went to the Shires to do, the Duke of Tyne clearly went for the hunting. Catherine harboured a suspicion that he might have been rather pleased to have a welcoming wife to come home to after a cold, wet day in the field.

She realized with a start that she must have been sitting in silence for some moments, for Sophie had started talking again.

"But I suppose it wouldn't have made any difference whether or not I had gone, because even during the summer I made these awful mistakes. I was never quite sure how I should go on. Mama told me I should appear to share his interests, and I would, you know, but she also said that I must not be too pushy or too coming. And she has never approved of ladies riding, and that was the only thing that Tony suggested we do together. I can ride, you know, but I didn't think that I should, at least not at the beginning. And now he doesn't even offer."

All this had been said in a low, fast voice. Now Sophie raised her head and looked at Catherine directly, with a look of determination on her pretty face. "I've rather started to wish that I hadn't listened to Mama before the wedding, because I see now that while she thought riding was unladylike, Tony does not. And it's the only thing he ever has cared I do. But now it's too late. He's given up on me, so it doesn't matter what I do."

7

THE EXPRESSION ON Sophie's face when she uttered these last words tore Catherine's heart open. "Do you really think so, Sophie?" she asked. "Surely—"

She would have continued, but Sophie interrupted. "Yes. Perhaps he never would have loved me the way I would like, but I think there was a time when we might have had something together. Because I do love him, you see. But I've ruined all that." She hesitated painfully. "I shouldn't say this, I know, but perhaps you'll understand. I daren't even write to Genie about it, because Mama would never forgive me if I did. It's not just that he's always going off and leaving me alone. He doesn't . . . he doesn't sleep with me any more, Caterina."

The miserable words out, she stared down at her intertwined fingers again, apparently intent on watching the way they writhed about each other.

Oh Lord, thought Catherine. How do I cope with this? Out loud she said only, "I see."

"And so that's how I know that it must be all over," Sophie said. "I think he must have given up on the marriage totally. Once or twice of late I've looked up and he's been watching me with this terribly miserable look on his face, as if he regrets that he ever married me. And I can't say that I blame him. I try very hard to behave as a duchess should, but you just have to look at his grandmother to see how far I fall short. But I wasn't brought up that way.

Really I wasn't. I was so happy when it was just the six of us in the country, and I miss Genie so much."

She paused, but not long enough for Catherine to make any reply. "Oh, Caterina, I'm so lonely," she continued in a rush. "I do wish Tony and I could have been friends at least. But that's how I got in the fix I'm in now. If I'd just met you before, but I didn't, so what's the good of repining?" This last was said with an air of determination, but it was followed almost immediately by a grimace.

"But, Caterina, what am I going to do about Sir William?"

Aha! thought Catherine. Out loud she said merely, "Do you need to do something?"

"He seems to think so," Sophie said earnestly. "It all started after Tony went away this last time. I was so miserable, because not only does it show that Tony really would rather be anywhere else but where I am, but I didn't have *anybody* to talk to then. At least when Tony's here I had him, but I daren't talk to Grandmother. I mean, would you?"

Catherine had to laugh, although her heart was wrenched with pity for this poor child. "Probably not, if she were my grandmama-in-law."

"Alec comes and talks to me sometimes, but he went off to Cumberland. Of all places to go! I mean, honestly. It's even worse than Northumberland. So when Sir William started showing me really the most flattering attention, I . . . I . . ."

"You paid some attention back. I can't say that I really blame you."

"I just wanted someone to talk to, Caterina, honestly. Somebody maybe I could laugh with a little bit. But apparently that wasn't what he had in mind at all. Really, honestly, I didn't mean to let him kiss me. But I did, just once, in an alcove at Lady Fotheringham's ball. And I liked it, too, in a way. It made me feel as if someone wanted me, but I knew I shouldn't let it go any further.

"And then I went to Lady Harrington's garden party, and he was so nice and gentlemanly that I went for a stroll with him. And . . ."

"He kissed you again," Catherine supplied.

"Something of the sort," Sophie said tearfully. "He said he loved me and that I was into this much too deep to start changing my mind now. That's when I ran away from him and you and Alec found me. I told him the next time I saw him, after you left that day when you and Alec were there, that we had to stop.

"But now Tony's come back, and it's clear he's regretting he married me. And Caterina, at least William does care for me." She looked directly at Catherine. "Don't mistake me. I don't think William loves me, not the way I love Tony. But he desires me, and that's better than nothing. Whenever I'm alone I start thinking, well, maybe it doesn't matter if I *am* into this too deeply to change my mind, because at least William's one person in the world who cares whether I live or die.

"Caterina, if I have to live the rest of my life with the only person who ever talks to me being that awful old woman telling me what to do, I don't think I can bear it. I honestly don't think I can bear it!" Her voice was still low, but it had risen in pitch to a low shriek. Her eyes were tearless now.

"And I'm not going to do so. I don't care. Other women do it, and I'm going to also. He's asked me to go to Vauxhall with him tonight, and I think I know what he has in mind then. And maybe Tony will discover and divorce me and then everything would be settled," she ended defiantly.

Catherine remained silent. It was one thing to have guessed something of Sophie's distress, quite another to hear it poured out to her in this kind of explicit detail. She had blithely set out to help Sophie, but was she equipped to do anything of the sort? Did she have any right to interfere in such a tangle, when she honestly could not see her way out of it? Her thoughts kept her speechless.

Finally, hesitantly, she said, "I think you're mistaken, Sophie. I watched the Duke when he was with you—"

"Then you don't know anything about it," Sophie flared. She jumped to her feet. "How dare you try to tell me that I'm wrong! Why does everybody seem to think they have some God-given right to do just that. I am sick to death of being told what to do. Why can't I be allowed to make even one decision on my own sometime."

"I thought you were asking for help," Catherine said mildly.

"Well, I wasn't. I was . . . oh, I don't know what I was doing and I don't care. I was a fool to talk to anybody." She turned and made for the door. "I was a fool to think that anybody would understand."

Helplessly, Catherine watched her leave. She had no idea what to do, and this was a novel feeling for her. The many crises that had filled her life had always had one common thread; one did what was necessary for personal survival. Moral decisions had always come second, and she had cheerfully lied, cheated, and occasionally even stolen, for the sake of all of their skins—her father, Jane, Pedro, herself. But this matter was something different, and she wasn't sure what she should do—or whether she should do anything at all.

Sophie had unquestionably confided in her under the impression that her confidences would be respected, and as such Catherine had no right to meddle, and certainly no right to repeat what she had been told, especially as her attempts to help had been repudiated. And yet . . . and yet. . . . She could not help hearing the cry for help that had existed behind every word of Sophie's speech. Surely if Sophie had truly wanted her confidences respected she would never have imparted them.

Catherine's thoughts whirled around in this circular fashion throughout the day, and continued to haunt her even as she was dressing for Almacks. For the first time, she found in herself an indifference to what she would wear that night, which for Catherine was as bad as Edmund Kean saying he didn't care whether they dressed him as Hamlet or Othello for the night's performance.

Jane watched with distress, and eventually—after stopping Catherine from donning a striking gold-embroidered spider gauze she had worn only the week before—demanded to know what was going on. "It's obvious that something's disturbing you, Cat," she said bluntly. "And I won't let you fret yourself over it."

After a moment's hesitation—very brief, for she never hid anything from Jane—Catherine told her.

"Well," said Jane. "My father was always used to say that God's way must be pursued at all costs, and he never held sacred anything that was confided to him if he felt that it was against the best interests of the individual or the community. I'm not sure I agree. I saw harm done that way many a time, but in this case I think he might be right. I have always believed it is the intent behind the words that counts. And there's no question in my mind that your little Sophie's intention was to ask for help, so I think you should give it to her. It's a pity that she didn't tell you what kind of help she had in mind, but there, we can't have everything. I doubt she knows herself."

"No," said Catherine vaguely, her attention having been distracted by Jane's rare reference to her childhood as the daughter of an English vicar. She seldom brought up such matters.

"I don't like the sound of Vauxhall at all," said Jane. "In my day it was always known as a place for assignations. There were a hundred little paths you could lose yourself down. Henry took me there once, and I am bound to say it was very romantic. All those floating paper lanterns, and the music . . . and the punch. I don't think we should discount the punch."

Catherine looked at her curiously. "Henry?"

"The father of my child," Jane said briefly.

"Oh," said Catherine. She knew, of course, that Jane had

borne a child out of wedlock, a child who had died just in time for Jane to become Catherine's wet nurse, but Jane seldom brought the matter up, and never before this specifically.

"I have wished occasionally that someone had stretched a helping hand out to me when I first met Henry," Jane said. "But then, of course, who am I to complain? Your father stretched a hand out to me in Paris, when the waters were about to close over my head, and you have been my life preserver ever since. Catherine, I should never have lectured you about involving yourself. Your little Sophie *needs* your help."

Catherine gave a little whimper of sympathy.

"I suppose we will just have to wait upon events," Jane said. "We don't even know that Sophie really plans to go to Vauxhall with Sir William. It might just be an idle threat. But there's such potential for disaster if she does, for God alone knows what he might persuade her to do in the mood she's in. I have known men like him, and I don't trust him. Well, see if Sophie is at Almack's tonight, and then make your decision."

Upon her arrival at Almack's Assembly Rooms a scant hour later, Catherine saw the Dowager Duchess of Tyne and her grandson the duke standing together, and was disturbed to note that Sophie did not appear to be with them. A quick glance around the room showed her Alec, looking very bored, dancing with a languid damsel garbed in pale pink with a wreath of flowers in her hair, but no sign of Sophie.

Purposefully, Catherine made her way around the floor towards the dowager and Tony. As she approached, the dowager raised a diamond lorgnette and regarded her through it. "Ah, Marchesa, I am glad to see you are honoring Almack's tonight. I am sure that Anthony would be delighted to dance with you."

Tony blushed a rosy red, but bowed very properly. "Would you do me the honour, Marchesa?" he asked.

Since a country dance was just forming, Catherine decided that this would be as good an opportunity as any to talk to him, and accepted his hand willingly. As they moved together and apart through the complex figures of the dance, she was able to determine that Sophie had stayed home with a headache.

"She's been looking poorly for days now, Marchesa, and when she came home from her morning calls today her eyes were red, as if she'd been crying," Tony confided suddenly. "I worry about her. I love her, you know, always have. She's such an adorable little kitten when she gets that big-eyed look of hers. That's why I asked her to marry me, but I think she only married me because that old dragon of a mother made her. And now I think maybe I shouldn't have married her, because she's clearly not happy."

The figures of the dance separated them, and Catherine was left to reflect on this sudden loquacity in the duke and on the confirmation of her guess.

When they met once more, Tony immediately started to speak again. "And whenever I ask her what's wrong she tells me it's nothing at all. I don't want to badger her, so I try not to ask too often. M'grandmother says she's a silly chit and probably sulking over some imaginary trifle, but I don't believe that."

They moved apart again, and Catherine sighed. Of such small matters were the webs of unhappiness woven. She was willing to lay odds that Sophie saw Tony's inquiries as nothing more than common courtesy, or even those of an irate spouse attempting to control his wife. But more pressing matters concerned Catherine now. It sounded as if Sophie had indeed gone to Vauxhall with Sir William, and Catherine had determined that she needed to do something about this matter. But what?

Mechanically she performed the steps of the "Sir Roger de Coverly" while she considered the matter. She had to go to the Gardens to find Sophie, and Heaven alone knew what she was going to find there, if Sir William had not already persuaded Sophie to leave for somewhere even more congenial to his purposes. She comforted herself that it was still early; presumably Sir William and Sophie would have only just arrived. Sir William was a gentleman with some style. He would wait an hour or two, would feed Sophie on shaved ham and rack punch, dance with her a few times.

Well, one thing was certain. She couldn't go on her own. An unescorted female would not get two yards before being accosted. She needed a male escort, which meant telling someone. She didn't seem to have much choice in the matter. Tony, as Sophie's husband, was undoubtedly the one whom convention dictated she should tell. But she was inclined to think this a mistake. The duke was clearly an honest, good-hearted soul; if he were to find Sophie in a compromising position, he might easily be willing to forgive her, but Catherine thought Sophie would never forgive herself.

And so, she realized, there was only one person—had always only been one person—who could help her. Mr. Carrock might be touchy, with an erratic temper that was easily exacerbated, but he combined a strong sense of family pride with an obvious affection for his cousin's wife. And, Catherine admitted, despite his occasional lack of subtlety, he exuded an air of calm competence that encouraged her to think that he might be of considerable help in a crisis.

Having made up her mind, she characteristically acted immediately. Time was of the essence. The last strains of the dance were coming to an end, and she curtsied in thanks to Tony. Looking around for Alec Carrock, she saw to her relief that he was standing alone. She hurried around the dance floor in an attempt to reach him before he moved elsewhere.

"Mr. Carrock," she said, "may I speak to you privately?"

A look crossed his face that was not so much one of surprise as it was of speculation and comprehension. "Certainly."

Placing her hand on his arm, she said in a low voice, "There must be somewhere we could speak in confidence for a few moments."

He nodded, and led the way towards a small, curtained alcove.

"I'll ruin your reputation," he said.

"As your grandmother would say, fiddlesticks. I have no reputation except one for bold eccentricity, which so far I seem to have been forgiven. This will merely serve to add to it."

He smiled. "You also have the reputation of being a beautiful, fascinating woman, very different from the usual milk-and-water miss we're treated to normally." His eyes were frankly admiring.

Despite the gravity of the moment, Catherine could not stop her heart from leaping. She cast a straight glance up at him. "Why, thank you, sir," she said lightly.

He pulled the curtain to the alcove aside with one hand, then replaced it behind them. "I meant it," he said, "but I don't think that's what you wanted to talk to me about. Not unless I'm much mistaken in you. I believe my cousin Sophie went to visit you this morning. Is this related?"

"You are very quick," she said admiringly. "Yes, it is."

"And the headache that she so unaccountably developed this evening is undoubtedly also related, is it not?"

"Yes," Catherine said, and quickly recounted for him those facts she thought it necessary he know. She tried to preserve Sophie's confidence as much as possible, only saying that she gathered there were problems between husband and wife.

Alec listened with attention, only occasionally stopping her to ask a pertinent question. When she was finished he said decisively, "As I presume you have already decided, you and I will have to go after the silly chit. I brought my phaeton, so as soon as we can have it poled up we'll be on our way."

The tone of his voice brooked no question or argument.

Catherine mutely resigned herself to following his directions. It was a novel experience for her, and not, she had to admit, a totally unpleasant one. After twenty-seven years of getting her father out of scrapes, there was a certain thrill in being told firmly what to do by a man who clearly had matters under control.

8

FIFTEEN MINUTES LATER, they were on their way to Vauxhall Gardens.

"Meysey probably took Sophie by water—she'd like that, silly little chit—but it's faster to take the bridge now that it has been opened," Alec had said authoritatively, and Catherine had agreed without a murmur.

With Alec's greys moving at a fast clip under his skilled control, they reached the newly constructed Vauxhall Bridge Road in minutes, and soon had turned onto the bridge itself. Here they hit obstruction, for the traffic was still, even at this hour, quite heavy, and the delay at the toll barrier considerable.

Catherine started to fidget, until Alec turned to smile at her with genuine warmth.

"Don't fret," he said. "Regardless of what you think, we've been here less than five minutes. I doubt my hen-witted cousin-in-law will have found time to do anything particularly stupid in five minutes." And he laid one warm hand over hers.

Catherine found his touch strangely reassuring, and he did not remove it until the way before them had cleared and he had to gather up the greys again.

In no time flat they were sweeping up to the entrance of the Gardens. Jemmy, the little tiger, jumped down from the back, and Alec told him to walk the horses, adding that he didn't know how long they would be. Alec then disbursed four shillings for the privilege of entering the gardens.

For the first time since Catherine had confided in him he showed signs of indecision. "Lord alone knows where the child will be," he said under his breath. "I suppose we're just going to have to wander around in the hopes of eventually finding them."

"I think we should try the area around the boxes first," said Catherine, "then extend our search to include the rest of the gardens."

"Have you any idea how big this damned place is?" Alec demanded with a note of petulance.

"No," Catherine admitted, "but you don't seem to have a better suggestion."

He laughed. "*Touché*. It's damn near eleven acres, actually, but you're quite correct, madame." He offered her his arm. "Shall we begin?"

Catherine placed her hand on his arm, and they commenced to wander casually along the first colonnade, which stood to the right of the entrance, peering into each of the small supper boxes that were interspersed along the colonnade as they did so.

"With my luck," Alec muttered, "we'll probably find married friends of mine with each other's spouses."

"Does that happen often?" Catherine asked.

"More than I'd care to indulge in. I suppose it's one reason I've never married. I have no intention of playing any woman false, and few women I know seem to hold the same beliefs. Look at Sophie, now. I can't say I blame the chit, under the circumstances, but there's a certain honesty I look for that I have never found in a woman."

He paused, then looked down at her with an arrested expression in his eyes. "Or, at least, a kind of honesty I had never thought to find in one of your sex. Since I met you I may have started to change my mind, Marchesa. There is something unusual about you, something straightforward and likeable, as if a man could be a friend with you."

Catherine found her heart was pounding painfully. Honesty? Marchesa? If he had any idea . . .

She forced herself to laugh. "*Merci du compliment, monsieur*," she said lightly. "I think we should walk up this colonnade here. We haven't tried it yet, have we?"

She had intended her remark to be flippant and dismissive, but the hurt on his face was so clear that she was hard-pressed to ignore it. Shame kept her quiet, however. How could she even think to accept a compliment she did not deserve? But to be his friend? How she wished she could.

In silence they toured each of the four colonnades, then wandered through the Grove in the central quadrangle and around the rotunda that housed the orchestra.

"They don't seem to be up here, do they?" Alec said crossly as they circled the Grove for the second time. "I think we're going to have to make a few passes down the walks."

Catherine smiled at his ill-temper, although she too was starting to be possessed of a sinking feeling that they had started on a wild goose chase. Together they strolled through the crowds that were thronging the long, tree-lined avenues and loudly admiring the fountains and cascades, whose waters glistened and sparkled in the light cast by the hundreds of lamps that lined the paths.

They turned up several more secluded paths, and occasionally stared rudely at an embracing couple, but none ever revealed themselves to be Sir William and Sophie. They strolled the Dark Walk, which Alec informed Catherine with some asperity was the one lane more than any other that had given Vauxhall its reputation as a lover's rendezvous—and certainly they passed any number of closely entwined pairs. They had nearly reached the end with a continued lack of success when Catherine noticed that Alec was regarding her oddly. She wondered at this, but a moment's consideration told her he must be worrying that they would never find Sophie. She hastened to reassure him.

"Just because we haven't seen her yet doesn't mean we won't find her if we keep trying," she pointed out.

"What?" Alec asked. He seemed genuinely puzzled. He recovered quickly, however. "Oh, yes. Sophie. No, no, I wasn't thinking of that."

"Well, then what were you thinking of," Catherine logically inquired.

"You don't want to know."

She was puzzled. "Why not?"

"Because I'm obviously suffering undue influence from an excessive number of couples behaving in a most immoral fashion in the middle of a public garden."

Catherine turned an innocently inquiring gaze up at him, but he seemed unwilling to continue further.

"Meaning?" she prompted.

He cast a hunted glance around, but finally returned his eyes to her. "Meaning that I was suddenly overcome by an urge to kiss you, if you're determined to know," he growled.

And that was when Catherine was seized by an urge most alien to the cautious nature she had so carefully instilled within herself over the years, to the prudence that had always been so necessary to counteract her father's intemperate flights of fancy. Richard was a creature of unconsidered whimsy; Catherine the model of care and forethought whose calm good sense had rescued them from many a sticky place. But now, after twenty-seven years of such good sense, her caution was deserting her, and the feyness that occasionally had to be stifled within her suddenly threatened to overwhelm her.

Why not give way to the impulse that seemed to have sprung fully-fledged into her head? Although, if truth be told, it was not an impulse entirely of the head, but rather one born of an indefinable mixture of the way Alec Carrock was looking down at her, and the breadth of his handsome shoulders, and the way his lips had felt on her wrist short days before. Why shouldn't she, for once in her careful life, do something mad and bad?

"Then why don't you?" she asked.

He groaned an answer.

She smiled up at him, an invitation on her lips. And then suddenly his arms were wrapped around her, pulling her firmly against the long, hard length of his body. Catherine felt a moment's dizziness, and in the flickering light of the distant gaslight saw the sculpted planes of his face, with the clear brown eyes and finely-drawn etched lips, swim above her.

And then he lowered those lips to hers, and the world was lost in a dizzying swirl of lamplit mist.

She moaned, and melted further into his embrace, aware of nothing but the kiss and the feel of his arms, like iron bands, pinning her soul to his.

When he finally raised his lips from hers, she swayed for a moment, uncertain where she was, unable to assimilate the cataclysm unlike any other that she had just experienced. She looked up at Alec, all her doubt and hope in her eyes.

"Well, Marchesa," he said drily. "I must congratulate you. You were right to give me a set-down earlier. How could I have insulted you by implying you possessed an honesty unlike a woman? You kiss quite as charmingly as you flirt. I hope you found English kisses as delightful as you found the English countryside."

She felt as if he had slapped her, and reacted just as she would have if he had hurt her physically. Unflinching, head held high, she faced him down, only the angry sparkle in her eyes betraying her hurt. How dare he? she seethed inwardly. How dare he imply that she collected kisses like some wretched souvenir? And yet, her sense of fairness asserted, could she blame the man? Every public word she had spoken, every public action she had taken for the last six weeks had been a lie. Each had been aimed with the express purpose of creating an illusion of a sophisticated, worldly-wise woman. She had never spoken of a lover, but hadn't her actions spoken louder? She had meant them to. Could she blame Alec Carrock for believing her as false as the image she projected? For not knowing she had never kissed a man before?

She smiled brilliantly. "Why, yes sir, I did. If you are to be your country's emissary, then I must admit you make a brilliant one."

He flushed, and seemed about to reply when a clear voice echoed from just around a corner.

"No, Sir William. I have changed my mind. I was a fool to come here with you."

There was a low baritone mutter in response.

"That's Sophie," said Catherine.

Alec didn't bother to reply, but whirled and charged around the corner, Catherine following hard upon his heels.

Sophie was backed up against a marble bench, but it was clear that she was as yet in control of the situation, for Sir William was maintaining a barely respectful distance of some few inches.

"Sophie," said Alec. "What are you doing here!"

Sophie turned her head. "Alec," she said with great aplomb. "And Caterina. So you too decided to take advantage of our lovely spring weather. How nice to meet you here."

Alec seemed about to explode. "Sophie—"

Catherine placed a hand on his arm, and he glanced at her. She raised a warning eyebrow and hurried into speech.

"It is lovely indeed, but it's getting late and I was just asking Mr. Carrock if he would take me home. Would you like to come with us, my dear Sophie?"

A glimmer of relief, hastily repressed, showed in Sophie's eyes. "That would be lovely. Are you leaving now?" Without waiting for an answer, she turned to Sir William. "I'm sure you wouldn't mind, would you, Sir William? It is getting rather late, and I'm sure Alec was planning on going up Upper Grosvenor Street anyway."

There was unmistakable annoyance on Sir William's dark face, but he did not allow it to appear in his manner.

"Of course. Heaven forbid that I should keep you from your sleep. Anything that would cause one less rose to bloom in your lovely cheeks would be most distressing."

Sophie laughed and linked her arm through Catherine's. "Why, Sir William, you are the most terrible flatterer. Come, Caterina, let us leave before he starts trying to turn your head as well." And despite the apparent frailty of her tiny frame, she almost forcibly propelled Catherine down the path, with Alec following in hot pursuit.

Catherine slept late the following morning, and spent most of the day puttering around the house aimlessly. She several times noticed Jane's worried eyes on her, so in the late afternoon she put on her oldest dress and retreated to the kitchen to help Teresa make ravioli.

The warm comfort of the kitchen, Teresa's friendly chatter in Italian, and the mindless repetition of the homely task of rolling out the pasta dough, filling it with Teresa's meat mixture, and then cutting it into little squares, served at last to slow somewhat the pace of her addled, confused thoughts.

She tried to concentrate on the laudable fact that she and Alec had retrieved Sophie unharmed, that while Sophie had seemed to be handling the situation with considerable aplomb, she had also clearly been extremely relieved to see Catherine and Alec, and that therefore the expedition had been a considerable success. But all her disordered thoughts seemed capable of dwelling on was the feel of Alec Carrock's long, muscled body against her own, the way her nerves had tingled as his face had hovered over hers, and the firm, soft touch of his lips.

Was this love? she wondered analytically. She, Richard's calm, cool Cat, was suddenly turned head over heels by some new and strange emotion. She thought another woman might call it love, but when others of her sex and generation had been reading the works of Ann Radcliffe, she had been reading Machiavelli and learning to fuzz a card. And yet, she had to admit that from the very beginning there had been some link between herself and Alec Carrock. A friendship, she thought. In some strange way, despite all her falsehoods, there had been between them the honesty of which he had spoken. And there lay the rub, for she found suddenly that she cared deeply for that honesty, and every step she took further would only drag her deeper into that morass of lies she had created.

She had come to a turning point in her life, she thought. She had undertaken this venture to London dancing as usual to Richard's piping. She had known what Richard hoped for her, known that the end result of this plan was that she deceive some man into marrying her. She had agreed to Richard's schemes, hoping in her heart that they would not come to fruition, believing she would find another way to remain in England. But she had agreed with open eyes.

And now she had come to the moment where a man could be, just possibly, persuaded to offer for her. Perhaps not, for Alec Carrock was made of firm stuff, and clearly held strong feelings on the subject of women.

Who could blame him for those feelings, she thought wryly, considering what his womenfolk put him through? I would not play him such a game if he were to offer for me.

Ah, but the game you would play him would be considerably worse, her inner self replied. You would trap him into a marriage that would be all a lie, for he would know nothing of the truth of you at all.

She sighed, and looked down at the pasta dough that she was twisting in her hands. With a grimace, she thumped it down onto the table. Teresa looked up, a question in her soft brown eyes.

"Have you ever been in love, Teresa?" Catherine found

herself asking, although that was not at all what she had thought she was about to say.

Teresa's puzzled look faded. "Ah," she said, "*amore*. Now I understand the way you mistreat my poor ravioli. Yes, once I was in love—quite desperately, I thought. He was an Englishman, a sailor, and I followed him here to London. But he left me, and if you had not taken me in, perhaps I would have starved. So now I know it is a mistaken thing to fall in love. For most of us, it will only lead to sorrow."

Was all love predicated on dishonesty? thought Catherine viciously, wielding a rolling pin with more vehemence than skill. If she were somehow to trap Alec into marriage, would she be any freer of guilt than Teresa's sailor?

"You're right," she said. "I should remember that."

If Catherine could have begged off the musicale she was due to attend that night, she would have. All her courage seemed to have deserted her, and she longed to turn tail and run. Her father waited in Calais. She and Jane could pack up in the night and leave. There were always greener pastures and new adventures, weren't there? That was the adventurers' dictum. But she was not the running type, and never before had she gone on to those greener pastures in a cowardly response to a paralysing fear. She was damned if she would do so now, even when faced with a dilemma far greater than any she had confronted before.

No, she had faithfully promised Lady Plymouth that she would come, and she would hold her head up high and go. Avoiding Jane's anxious looks, she donned her most clinging, revealing dress, daringly damped her petticoats, and departed. She did not know if she was relieved or disappointed to find that Alec Carrock was not in attendance. She arrived home late, slept badly, and at eleven the next morning was still sipping coffee in a lackluster way in the breakfast parlor, Jane having already stepped out to make a few purchases.

When the doorbell rang, she ignored it, for she had told Bagwell to deny her to any callers, so she was surprised to hear shortly after the unmistakeable evidence of an altercation. Even in her present troubled mood, Catherine's curiosity remained her one overwhelming vice, so she stepped into the hall to discover what was going on.

An unusually rumpled-looking Alec Carrock was besieging her portals. It looked as if he had tied his cravat with his eyes shut, and she strongly suspected that he had not brushed his hair. Her foolish heart gave a thud when she saw him—even his dishevelment had an unusually touching quality, she found—but it was clear that Alec had other matters on his mind.

"Good morning, Mr. Carrock," she said calmly.

He greeted her appearance with extreme relief.

"Caterina, thank heaven you're here. Sophie's bolted."

"What?" Catherine's mind didn't seem to be working very well this morning. Perhaps, she thought, she hadn't absorbed enough coffee yet.

"Bolted. Gone. Taken off with that blighter Meysey."

Catherine's eyes snapped wide-open for the first time that morning. Her worries and concerns of the previous day vanished in the face of this new challenge. "Oh, *diable*. How do you know?"

"She wrote me a letter, of all things. Why me? That's what I'd like to know."

"Because she trusts you, Alec." Instinctively, Catherine followed his lead and used his given name. Somehow, in this shared conspiracy, their relationship seemed to have progressed to such an informality, and the awkwardness that had ended their previous meeting was at least temporarily forgotten. "You're the only one in London who's shown her real sympathy, I think."

"Except you," he pointed out.

"Except me, I suppose," she said. "But why did you come to me with this news?"

"Because I didn't have a blasted notion what to do. And

I thought that maybe you could help me." He sat down on a convenient chair that stood against the wall of the hallway, dropped his head to his hands, and groaned. "What am I going to do with the chit? I suppose I'm going to have to go after her and rescue her. Why doesn't Tony take care of his own wife?"

"Well, I think this time he should," said Catherine decidedly.

Alec's head jerked up. "What?"

"I think the duke *should* be taking care of his own wife."

He stared at her as if she had lost her senses.

"Well, it's clear the two of them are hopelessly in love," Catherine pointed out. "I don't know if either has ever seen fit to confide in you, but I can assure you that both idiots have made plain to me their hopeless and unrequited passion for the other. Do you have Sophie's letter with you?"

Alec produced it, and Catherine scanned it quickly. It was yet another of Sophie's unmistakable epistles, swinging between the breathless and the verbose, and most erratically capitalized.

> Dearest Alec,
>
> How Devastating to have to write this, but I am Fleeing with Sir William Meysey. I Know that You and my Dearest Caterina promised that you would never Breathe a word to a soul of my Unfortunate Indiscretion at Vauxhall Gardens, but how can you Keep such Improper Behavior from my poor Husband? Surely your Conscience would have Overcome you and you would have felt Required to tell him. In Fact, I would have held you Guilty of the most Uncousinly behavior if you had Not. So you see I have no Choice but to Flee these Shores.
>
> Sir William, as you may Know, is under Pressing Monetary Obligation to Depart this Country for some Period of Time, and has been most

Insistent in his Persuasions that I should Accompany him. I had told him Last Night when you Came upon me that I could do No such Thing, but now I see that it is Almost my Duty to Do So. By the Time you Read this we will be nearly to Dover. Please do Not try to Follow me, and please tell Tony that he must Divorce me and Marry Another. I am Sure that the Duchess can Find Many far More Suitable than

Sophie

Postscriptum. I have taken little Valancourt with Me, so None need Worry about him Either.

9

CATHERINE HANDED THE letter back in silence, finding that she was hard-pressed to know whether to laugh or cry at this effusion. It was as overemotional and ridiculous as Sophie always was, yet there was an undercurrent of truth that tugged at her heartstrings. She looked up to see Alec's eyes glistening.

"Pretty pathetic, ain't it?" he said. "I hate to think of the poor little child roaming Europe with that lecher. He's hot for her now, that's obvious, but will he stay that way now she's no longer playing hard to get? How long will he even bother to keep her under his protection if we let her flee the country with him? I hate to think of her abandoned somewhere when he tires of her."

Catherine thought of Jane, to whom exactly that had happened. If Richard had not come along at the right moment, with a squalling baby in need of a wet nurse, who knew what depths Jane would have fallen to? And while Catherine suspected that Sophie possessed hidden depths of resilience few saw, even the strongest was unlikely to survive such an experience without luck of the kind Jane had encountered. Catherine shuddered.

"Alec, we can't keep hiding this from the duke," she said firmly. "You can see for yourself that that is why she has fled now. She fears how he will react if he hears, which she thinks is certain. And I tend to agree with her. Affairs of this type can never be kept a secret for long. I meant the very best when I persuaded you to go to Vauxhall with me, but I was mistaken. We may have precipitated a tragedy by finding her there."

Alec opened his mouth as if to protest, but Catherine shook her head decisively. "No. I think we both were mistaken. Only if we can persuade the Duke to tell her himself that he loves her and wants her back are we going to be able to retrieve this situation. We have to tell the duke."

"Oh, Lord," said Alec. "Sooner you than me."

"I think I have a plan," said Catherine. "You and the duke will have to go to Dover immediately, and we must hope that they have not already taken ship."

"I think maybe not," said Alec. "You haven't been outside today, I take it. There's a howling great gale out there. I doubt there'll be a ship put out for at least a day." Suddenly his harassed face lightened in a grin. "Trust Sophie. Only she would try to escape to the Continent in a blasted hurricane."

Catherine laughed. "Well, we can only hope. Will you be able to drive in it?"

"I've never seen weather that could stop me yet," he said with confidence.

"Then I need to tell you what my plan is." Catherine said.

Alec's phaeton was pulled up in front of Tyne House, the little tiger Jemmy holding the eager greys with difficulty. Catherine stood in the doorway, warmly wrapped in a wool pelisse against the late spring gale that whipped up the trees and sent gusts hurtling around her ankles. Outside on the steps stood Alec, tapping his leather driving gloves, which he held in one hand, impatiently against one hard thigh.

He was dressed practically for driving in inclement weather, but Catherine found she could not help thinking how well the tight-fitting whipcord breeches, the glossy topboots, and the unfastened many-caped driving coat suited his slim, taut-muscled physique. The wind was tumbling his brown curls into wild disorder even as she watched, and the grim line in which his lips were set only emphasized the classical regularity of his handsome features.

He turned, and caught her looking at him. A brief smile crossed his features, and he started towards her, as if he would say something. Then footsteps sounded on the stairs behind her, and his attention was distracted.

"Tony, are you ready?"

"Yes," said the duke, an unusual look of determination on his pleasant features. He turned to Catherine. "I want to thank you, ma'am, for your help. I only hope that we can recover my wife in time. If we can, then perhaps all my mistakes of the last year can be rectified. I am not very good at expressing myself to women, but perhaps if I am extremely lucky I can some day teach Sophie how to love me."

Catherine laughed. "You could try telling her what you've just said to me."

Tony's face softened. "I will never forget how little and defenseless she looked that first day I saw her at Almacks. I knew then I had to have her for my wife. But I've never known how to tell her that."

"Just tell her," Catherine said. "And, Duke, one word of advice?"

He nodded.

"Get her away from your grandmother."

"Ma'am, nothing would please me better. You may have noticed I spend most of my life trying to do the same thing m'self."

Alec tapped him on the shoulder. "Tony, the horses are going to bolt down the street if we leave them with poor Jemmy much longer. Caterina, good-bye. With any luck I'll see you tomorrow. I'll come by Portman Square as soon as I can. Come on, Tony." And he swept the duke down the steps and into the phaeton.

Catherine stood watching as he gathered up the reins. The horses sprung forward, little Jemmy jumped for his perch in back, and they swept off down Grosvenor Street towards Waterloo Bridge and the Dover Road. Catherine remained watching until she had lost them from view.

In early afternoon of the next day, Catherine was sitting at the window looking over Portman Square. A hat she was supposedly trimming lay in her lap, but her hands were as idle as they had been for most of the morning, and her gaze remained glued to the square below her. When a hackney appeared, she did not immediately notice. She was watching, as she had been all morning, for Alec Carrock's phaeton and greys. But then the hackney stopped in front of her house and Alec himself climbed out. Catherine threw the hat across the room, and ran for the door, arriving there just after Bagwell.

"Did you find her?" she called around the stolid butler.

"Success!" Alec cried. He swirled past Bagwell and swept Catherine up into an embrace that sent her feet flying from the ground and her heart flying into her mouth, then put her down again and stood grinning at her.

"You're a genius, Caterina! All occurred exactly as you predicted. How did you know?"

Catherine was still shaken and breathless from the embrace. "I didn't know. I just hoped. Everything? Where are the duke and Sophie?"

"Halfway to Tyne by now, I hope. Or actually, I hope not. I escorted their hired post chaise as far as the turnoff for the road to Northumberland. If they have any sense at all they're in the best inn on the Great North Road, asking the landlady for the best set of rooms."

"That sounds promising," said Catherine. "What happened?"

"Well, much of this we reconstructed afterwards, but it pretty much went as follows. We caught up with them in Dover. Just as I'd hoped, the wind had remained high, and one glance at the whitecaps kicking up in the harbor was enough to tell us that they wouldn't have left. We found them at the inn there.

"They'd travelled all night, and apparently by the time they'd reached Dover Sir William had managed to insult Valancourt three times and kick him once. I'm sure the kick was accidental, and probably the insults were as well, but try telling Soph that. I've certainly never been successful under similar circumstances, and it's clear that Meysey had no concept of how to handle her.

"So dear little Sophie had apparently upped and told the landlord that they were brother and sister and needed two rooms. I gather Meysey was trying to persuade her otherwise, but of course by this time the landlord was violently suspicious, which I can assure you was not improving dear Sir William's temper.

"And despite the fact that by the time we arrived the two of them must have already been in Dover for a number of hours, it was clear the minute we walked into the inn that Sir William and Sophie were still in the midst of a flaming row. You could hear them going at it hammer and tongs clear down in the public room. So I grab the innkeeper and tell him that Tony is the lady's husband, and we bolt upstairs. All the way up we can hear Sir William yelling, and Sophie crying, and, of course, dear little Valancourt running around madly and yapping, which I doubt was improving Sir William's temper one little bit.

"So there's Sophie, perched on the most damned uncomfortable chair you ever saw, crying her little heart out over some imagined insult to Valancourt. I open the door and see this, so I immediately grab Tony, who's trying to hide behind me, and shove him into the room.

"And Tony, bless his soul, for once in his life does the right thing at the right time. He just walks right in and opens his arms wide and says very quietly 'Sophie.' And she looks up and you've never seen anything like the expression on her face. She bolts into his arms and starts crying down his waistcoat. So Tony picks her up and carries her from the room with her arms twined around his neck, leaving me to deal with Sir William—which I must admit I did with a certain amount of pleasure."

Alec paused and glanced down at the knuckles of his right hand. "His nose is going to be very sore for a number of days, I think."

Looking up at Catherine again, he grinned. "And that's about the sum of it."

Catherine was laughing and crying at the same time. "Oh, Alec, I'm so glad. I'm so glad. I hoped, I really hoped."

"But how did you know? How could you have guessed that this would be the way of it?"

"Well, Alec, honestly. Have you ever been anywhere with Sophie when she hasn't created a scene of that kind? I didn't know it would be Valancourt who would cause the problem, although I should have guessed, but it was inevitable that something would. Sophie's always in alt over something. And since both Sophie and the duke have confided to me on separate occasions their unalterable passion for each other, I could only hope that she would be upset enough to throw herself weeping into his arms, and that he—"

She broke off, considered what she had been about to say, and decided to continue to be honest. "Excuse me if I'm being rude about your cousin, but I have never seen a man more hopeless with women. Does he only know how to talk to those females that have four legs and a tail? Anyway, I could only hope that the duke would for once have the instinctive sense to comfort her. Which I gather she did and he did. So there you have it. Rather simple, really."

Alec was looking at her with awe. "Simple when you put it that way, perhaps. But I don't notice that any of us who should have been watching out for Sophie had tumbled to it. Caterina, I think my family owes you the deepest of thanks."

His words should have sent a glow of pleasure and a sense of a task well accomplished through Catherine, and indeed she was happy for the sake of Sophie and her duke. But now that the excitement was over, she found she was suffering from a return of conscience. It was abominable how she was treating this poor trusting family, and it was especially terrible how she was treating Alec Carrock, who was clearly coming to like and trust her.

Alec looked around the hall, as if to see whether Bagwell, who had discreetly disappeared some ten minutes earlier, was still present.

"Caterina," he said, and the look in his eyes was warm.

Catherine found that the shared excitement of Sophie's elopement had made her decision for her. She could not encourage this man to consider a marriage that she would know to be based on falsehoods. And judging from the look in his eyes, she thought that he was starting to hold a warmth of feeling for her. Which meant that she must quickly put paid to any intimacy between them.

"La, sir," she said gaily. "It was nothing. Your cousin Sophie is a charming child, and I hope I can count her as a friend of mine. It was interesting to see what happened."

The warmth disappeared in a flash from Alec's face as the lightness of her tone penetrated. He stared at her. "Something to enliven the boredom of your day, I suppose," he said roughly.

"Exactly," said Catherine.

He flushed a deep red. His tone when he spoke was as icy as it had been when they had first clashed so many weeks ago. Catherine flinched inwardly.

"Well, I'm glad we could be of service in such a way, ma'am," he said. "But I must be going now. It's been quite some while since I've seen my bed."

Suddenly, now that the excitement was over, his tiredness seemed to show in the slump of his shoulders and the lines of his face. Some deep, illogical part of Catherine longed to comfort him, to hold his head against her breast and soothe him to sleep. Instead, she smiled brightly.

"My dear Mr. Carrock, I am sure that you must have a tiredness the most incredible, so I will forgive that last ill-tempered remark. I am only glad that I could in my own poor way help the little Sophie." She held out a hand dismissively. "Please tell me if you hear from her. I hope that all will be happy for her and her duke."

Alec bowed correctly. "Of course. Ma'am, your devoted servant."

He turned and walked slowly down the steps to the waiting hackney. Catherine stood looking after it as it disappeared around the corner, a feeling of emptiness slowly spreading through her. Despite the worry over Sophie, she had enjoyed the last few days unlike any other time in her life. The intimacy she had shared with Alec Carrock had been different, special. In her lonely life, there had never been anyone but her father and Jane. And now, for the first time, she started to wonder if that was enough.

10

SIR WILLIAM MEYSEY sat in his rooms on Half Moon Street with a pile of crumpled bills in front of him, assessing his financial situation. His dark, saturnine face grew progressively grimmer as he read each amount listed. He knew, of course, that he should have continued to the Continent even after Alec Carrock and the Duke of Tyne had caught up with him. It not only made sense from a financial point of view, but if he'd had any pride at all, he would have played the part of the devil-may-care man-about-town, and gone to Venice with or without the woman.

But the hell of it was that he did care. It had only been in the last few years that he had slowly come to realize how little of its early promise life had vouchsafed him. Twenty years ago he had been an eager boy, the proud possessor of a title, a fine house and profitable estate, a comfortable fortune. Life had seemed well worth living then. The excitement of hunting with boon companions, the flirtations with pretty women, the dances, the musicales, the intimacy of his friends at White's and Brook's, the thrill of a long night of winning at dice or cards, of a long day of backing the right horse at Newmarket.

That thrill was the only pleasure still left him. When the cards or the horses ran right, then he could still recapture the exuberance of his youth. But it seemed that as his money dwindled he won less frequently. Or was it the other way around? No matter. The right turn of cards, always a bright, beckoning spirit, had become more and more elusive, and the growing pile of dunning letters and the dwindling of his credit were only the most superficial measure of his corresponding desperation.

And then, just when his life had seemed at lowest ebb, he had met Sophie, Duchess of Tyne—newly wed and just as newly abandoned by her husband. He had a way with women—with pretty bored young matrons as much as with the barques of frailty who had slowly started to abandon him as the money available to squander on them grew less—and he had never lacked for a flirt of the week or month. But little Sophie, with her pale, porcelain beauty and her shy, affection-hungry, elusive response to his advances, had captured him in a way he had never known before, until he had come to see her as some personification of Lady Luck, always just ahead, always beckoning. He had become convinced that when she was finally his, then his luck would change.

And it had been so near. Her pale, perfect beauty had been within his grasp. She had agreed to go with him to Venice, where his acquaintance, Marc Antonio d'Amici, kept one of the most profitable gambling houses in Europe. Marc Antonio had promised him a partnership, one in which William's knowledge of and intimacy with the English aristocracy who were now starting to make their way back to Italy would have balanced Marc Antonio's established venture. It would have been a comedown in the world for Sir William Meysey of Meysey Manor, but the thought of making money off men as pitiful as himself had had a charm of its own. All had been set in train.

But then he had lost Sophie, and with her he knew he had lost his luck. In time, he would have to leave off skulking like a whipped dog here in England, for his creditors would not give him much longer. He supposed he would join Marc Antonio as planned. But without Sophie, his Lady Luck, it would not be the same.

With a low growl of rage, Sir William stood, giving the table an impatient push as he did so. The pile of accumulated bills went flying, and he slammed his fist on the table in frustration.

Damn them. Damn them. Damn them!

Damn Sophie, and damn her husband, who had never before shown any sign of wanting her.

And damn Alec Carrock, who had clearly been the reason the duke had bothered to retrieve his wife.

And damn most of all that nosy, interfering Italian woman, in whom William strongly suspected Sophie had confided. Nobody in Tyne's family had bothered about Sir William in the least before the di Carabas woman had shown up. The first sign of any interest on their part at all had been that night at Vauxhall. The di Carabas woman had been much in evidence there, and Sir William did not believe that Alec Carrock was the kind of man who would have gone to a woman for help. No, she had clearly been the instigator of the venture, and he could track the downfall of his enterprise from that moment.

Damn her. If only there were some way of getting his revenge on her. He struck the table again.

And then he smiled—a bitter, grim smile. Perhaps there was a way. A rogue can recognize a rogue, he thought. This marchesa had always struck him as a suspicious character, appearing out of the blue as she had, queening it around society, smiling sideways out of those green cat eyes. Who knew what the truth about her might be? And just one piece of dirt would be enough to ruin her in society.

With the smile still chasing around the corners of his mouth, he fetched ink and a pen.

Dear Marc Antonio, he wrote.

He paused, considering, and chuckled.

"So what are your plans, Catherine?" Jane asked.

"Plans?" Catherine looked up from the pale pink feathers she was carefully attaching to a white straw bonnet. May had brought with it the promise of summer. To Catherine, used to the warmth of more southern climes, it seemed extremely chilly still, but fashion dictated that everyone now appear in the lightest of muslins and spider gauzes, and hats were needed to match.

"Yes, Catherine. Plans. I've never known you this distracted. You seem to be letting this venture of yours coast. When are you going to send word to your father?"

Catherine studied the feather she was presently stitching to the bonnet, as if she had to determine the exact placement. She knew she was not fooling Jane, but she dared not let her eyes meet those of the older woman. In truth, she had few plans. She had known a moment of decision when she had dismissed Alec Carrock so finally, but it seemed to elude her now. His formal, chilly bows when they were inadvertently thrown together struck her to the heart, and she found herself torn between a stricken conscience and a determination not to turn and run. She was conscientiously fulfilling the day-to-day role of the Marchesa di Carabas, but she knew that soon she would need to do more. Her father was still in Calais, waiting for the word from her that would summon him for his role in the adventure. But to summon him would be to open herself to his scheming, and that she could not seem to bring herself to do.

"I don't know," she said finally. "Don't snap at me, Jane dear. The time just doesn't feel right yet. I must wait for the right moment." She sighed, and bent her head to her sewing again, as if to ward off any more conversation.

Jane looked at her searchingly. She couldn't seem to fathom her girl, the child she had raised from infancy, these days. There was something distressing Catherine. Something that was distracting her from the matter at hand.

"Have you seen Mr. Carrock recently, dear?" she asked finally, drawing a bow at a venture.

"No, should I have?" asked Catherine frigidly.

"I was wondering how little Sophie was doing."

Catherine's face softened, as it couldn't help but do when Sophie's name was mentioned. "You saw the letter from her. She seems ecstatic now that Tony and she have finally learnt to talk to each other. I shouldn't wonder if we'll hear of an heir to the duchy on the way any day now. And I did see the dowager duchess briefly yesterday. I don't know that she'll ever forgive me completely for my meddling, but she does have to admit that even the Verlains could not have managed to survive the scandal if Sophie had eloped successfully with Sir William. So she's been guardedly polite. She talked of inviting me to a small card party in two weeks, but I don't know I'll be able to attend."

"And why not?" asked Jane roundly, as if Catherine were still her little nursling. "I thought that's what you were here for."

Because Alec might be there, and I can't bear to face his disdain, yet dare not encourage anything else, Catherine cried silently. But she turned a stony face to Jane and refused to reply, as she had all too often in the last few weeks when sensitive subjects were touched upon. And as she had often of late, Jane watched her and worried, but said nothing.

A letter arrived from Italy. Returning home one morning after a night at Brooks, Sir William Meysey pounced upon it, ripping the wrapper off. He scanned the closely scrawled writing with attention, and an expression of triumph grew on his face.

Every so often he exclaimed softly to himself, and finally, after finishing the epistle, he said in a low voice, "By damn, I think I've trapped her!"

> My dear Marchesa, I have a communication for you that you might find of interest. Please meet me in my rooms at Number 15 Half Moon Street at ten o'clock tonight. If you value your own interests, you will tell no one and come alone.
>
> Yours, etc., Meysey.

Catherine crumpled the note in her hand as she walked up and down the room, considering. For the first time in weeks, she felt her blood racing in her veins, driving away the awful lassitude that had paralyzed her of late. Twenty-seven years of dangerous living had taught her to scent danger, and even a baby would have recognized a threat in the last line of this letter.

Her eyes sparkling, she sought out Jane.

"Don't go," Jane said.

"I have to. He's clearly bubbled us, and I have to find out how badly. Does he just suspect, or does he know something? I confess to a very bad feeling about this, Jane."

"So do I," Jane said. "Are you sure we shouldn't just cut our losses and run? You can't win every time, my dear. Think how often your father has said that."

It was the perfect excuse. Richard would be disappointed if they left now, but not surprised. She would never have to explain about Alec Carrock, or her own crisis of conscience. But her blood was singing in her veins like fire, and the clear-cut challenge had finally sent all doubt flying from Catherine's mind.

"Oh, we haven't lost yet," she said cheerfully. "Let me scout out the enemy first."

Jane looked as if she would have liked to argue the point, but it had never been her place to act as more than advisor, so she remained quiet and grudgingly acquiescent.

At nine-thirty that evening, Catherine, dressed in a serviceable twill walking dress, stepped quietly out of the kitchen door. If she had known for certain that Sir William was aware of her true identity she would have worn her man's attire. Not only would it have given her more freedom of movement, but she could also have carried her sword cane. As it was, she had to be content with the knowledge of the small, serviceable pistol hidden in the pocket of the dress. She hoped she wouldn't have to use it, but she always prepared for contingencies. She had warned Jane to be ready for a hasty departure if need be.

But while she was careful to prepare for the worst, excitement was bubbling within her. She had selected her dress for its wide-cut skirt and plain lines, but her sense of drama had also played a part in her choice. She disdained any impression of cowardice or skulking, and the dress she had chosen was a rich burnt orange that was only made the more striking by its lack of frills and furbelows. Over it, she had wrapped a mannishly cut caped driving coat of dark wool. She planned to walk, and with her long, unfeminine stride, she hoped that in the darkness she would be mistaken for a man and left undisturbed.

Half Moon Street was reached without incident, and when she knocked firmly on the door at the upstairs landing, Sir William himself answered it.

"Ah, Marchesa," he said, smiling. "I hope you don't mind my informality. I have let my man go for the evening. I thought it best to have absolute privacy. I believe my landlady is also out."

Catherine felt a chill of excitement run through her. "As you wish, Sir William," she said calmly.

He closed the door behind her. "Sherry, my dear Marchesa?"

"No, thank you. I think we should get to the point immediately."

"As you wish, Miss Catherine Brown. And how is your charming father Richard? I am surprised that he has not as yet put in an appearance in our delightful city."

It was worse than she had supposed. He might be only drawing a bow at a venture, but it was clear that he knew far more than he should. Whether or not she confirmed his suppositions, she was ruined in London.

"You are very well-informed, sir," she said calmly.

"I try, my dear."

"I wonder how."

"I have a friend in Venice—the owner of an exclusive gaming establishment called Marc Antonio's."

"I see," said Catherine. She did see. Richard had been very fond of Marc Antonio's. He had good luck there, and had gained some notoriety. Catherine herself had met Marc Antonio several times.

"Shall we say that I had always had my suspicions, my dear?" said Sir William. "Who you were was no concern of mine, however, until you put paid to my aspirations with the little Duchess of Tyne. Then I wrote a letter to my friend Marc Antonio, asking whether he had ever heard of the Marchesa di Carabas. In case that name did not ring a bell with him, I also enclosed a full description of you."

His dark, cynical gaze held hers. "A beautiful woman, I said, with slanted green eyes and dark gold hair." He paused, and allowed his eyes to run openly over her body, then added insolently. "And a body that would make any man want her for his bed. Curves that cry out to be fondled, and breasts not so full that they couldn't be cupped easily in a man's hand.

"Marc Antonio recognized the description immediately. I gather he had hopes of you for his bed himself, and I can't say that I blame him. But you disappeared too soon. I gather there was trouble with your father and a cuckolded husband. Marc Antonio was not surprised to hear you had appeared in London under another name, although I gather he finds it odd that I had no word of your father."

He paused, and eyed Catherine expectantly.

"So why did you ask me here?" she said. "It doesn't matter whether this information you think you have is true or not. By the time I could summon proof from Venice of my credentials as the Marchesa di Carabas, I would have lost all appeal to London society. You can ruin me easily now. Your story could be a complete fabrication, but it's a clever one, and who here in London would care whether it was true or not? The scandal would be all that anybody cared about. Perhaps you think I will pay you to keep quiet. If so, you are greatly mistaken."

"I asked you here because merely ensuring that you are discredited in London society is not sufficient for me. I want you to feel real pain, pain such as I felt when your interference cost me Sophie. If you had not come, then I could have circulated my rumors. It would have been something. But you did come. And I think you will find that you have made a great mistake."

"Do you?" asked Catherine coolly, as if academically interested. "Why?"

"Because, as I mentioned earlier, we are alone here tonight. Because I am probably a great deal stronger than you. And because I want something in return for what I lost when you queered my game with the Duchess of Tyne."

Catherine, watching him, noted that the glint in his eye was not that of a totally sane man, and for the first time she felt a quiver of fear. But fear was not an emotion that she had ever found to be very constructive, so she did not let it take over now. She had once or twice been in a worse situation, she thought, but not often. There was the pistol in her pocket, and she could hope that Sir William did not know enough about her to be expecting that, but she knew he was counted to be a fast, deadly shot himself. She thought that she would not try the pistol yet.

"What did you have in mind?" she asked.

"What Sophie was about to give me when Tyne and Carrock turned up."

Catherine felt a flash of anger. "I gather she wasn't," she said before she thought.

He flushed a dark red. "Damn you, woman," he said in a low, deadly voice.

He moved more quickly than she expected, and had grabbed her arms before she could think of her next move. "She would have," he grated. "She had said she would. You stole her from me, and I want something from you in return. I want to make you suffer." He lowered his head in a hard, abusive kiss.

The pain nearly made tears spring to her eyes, but Catherine knew there was no point in fighting him at this moment. She was a strong woman, but Sir William had undoubtedly spoken the truth when he had said he was stronger than she. Although she made sure that she always remained muscled and fit, clearly he did so as well, and he had six inches of height and probably fifty pounds of weight on her. A wrestling match was not going to come out in her favor, and with his hands grasping her upper arms, attempting to reach her gun would merely serve to warn him that she had one.

Catherine forced herself to discard her repugnance and relax into the embrace, her mind working furiously all the while. She thought it extremely unlikely that he would actually manage to rape her. At some point he would relax his guard. A man cannot be fully alert when he is unfastening his trousers and she thought he seemed a little overly sure of himself. She thought she would be able to liberate her gun at that point, and that would give her a sufficient advantage to be able to take her leave.

But if she did that, then she had guaranteed the downfall of her London adventure. Richard would be incredibly disappointed, and she, she found that her mettle had been roused. She was damned if she would give in so easily to this slimy bastard.

Sir William raised his head, and she saw a look of faint disappointment. He had wanted her to struggle, she realized. Her acceptance of his kiss had taken the edge off his sense of power.

Feeling her way through the problem, she plastered a gay smile to her lips and ran a light finger down his cheek. She remembered Alec Carrock's painful words not so many nights before. Well, she could play the adventuress as well as she could the marchesa. "La, sir," she said, "I've known a few men in my day, and not many have been your equal."

The disappointment in Sir William's eyes increased.

"Perhaps it would not be so bad a fate to lie with you, if that was what I had to do to win my freedom." The words seemed to be spoken by another person. All the time she was thinking furiously. There had to be a weak spot. What was this man's weakness? And then she remembered his reputation as a man who would gamble on anything. She remembered the intensity he had shown when he was betting on the frogs in the pond at Richmond. And she thought about her own ability at piquet. She almost never lost, and she was a gambler herself.

"But I have better proposal for you. Are you willing to take a wager?"

"A wager?" he asked.

"I'm accounted not a complete novice at piquet. Three hands of piquet, and the winner takes all. My stakes are the following. If you win, I not only bed you now, but if you wish I will come with you to the Continent as your mistress. If I am to be ruined here, it would not be so bad a fate." She shuddered inwardly at the thought, and knew that if she lost she would use the gun yet. But she almost never lost.

"And what should my stakes be?" asked Sir William, and Catherine realized with a thrill of terror that she had hooked him.

"I ask only that if I win that I be allowed to leave, and that you will hold your tongue about me."

He frowned. "The stakes appear uneven. It seems to me that you are gambling everything you have. I never gamble for uneven stakes."

"What do you want to wager?"

"What good to me is a house ridden by debt? In a country I will be no longer living in? If you gamble everything, so will I. I'll throw in Meysey Manor as well, although I warn you the land's been sold long since. Why should I care about a house that I barely see? Is that fair, Miss Brown? Your body against the last of my inheritance."

"Fair," said Catherine, concealing her surprise. She had thought the man to have a harder head than this, but she supposed that this was the difference between a gambler and an adventurer. A little matter like uneven odds had never disturbed her. And she had no intention of standing by her wager if she lost. She had a suspicion that this man would.

"But we'll play only one hand," he said suddenly, as if the thought had just come to him. "I've never liked long games. I prefer to risk everything on one venture."

Catherine cursed inwardly. The three hands she had suggested favored skill. One hand gave far more of an edge to chance. Well, she supposed she would play his game. She did not, when all was added up, have much choice in the matter, and if the luck would only remain fairly even, skill would win the game.

"Fair," she said again, and held out her hand.

He took it, then walked away to another room, returning with an unopened pack of cards. He moved a candelabra from the desk to a card table that stood in one corner of the room, and pulled out a chair.

"Miss Brown?"

11

THE LIGHT OF the manic gambler was already in Sir William's eyes, Catherine saw. That was good. Men such as he was did not consider the odds as coolly as she, a professional, would. She smiled thinly, concealing her very real fear under the mask she had learned years ago to adopt when she was most afraid.

They drew for the deal, and Sir William held the lower card, which meant he was the dealer, or major, for the first round. That was bad, for the advantage was with the dealer in this game, but they had to reach a hundred points. Unless she were very unlucky, they would play more than one round, and the deal would come round to her yet.

Sir William dealt the twelve cards each swiftly and surely. It was clear, though this came as little surprise to Catherine, that he was very familiar with the game. She considered her cards with a still face, then made her discard carefully.

When Sir William made no discard at all, she guessed that he had made carte blanche, and cursed silently, although she thought no such expression appeared on her face. That meant an automatic ten points for him. Well, good luck early sometimes made an opponent cocky. She could only hope that would happen here.

Alternating, they called the rest of their scores on that hand, then played through the tricks. Sir William, as Catherine had guessed he would, came out slightly ahead but not, she thought, significantly so.

He shot her a look of triumph, and she smiled, but allowed a slight expression of nervousness to show. Let him think he had all the advantage. It would make him careless, and piquet was far more a game of skill than it was of luck. It took a certain coolness of temperament, a good memory, and a keen mathematical talent to play well, and experience counted in the balance. She thought Sir William believed that his age and sex gave him an advantage. She was laying odds that it did not.

Unless he had a far different childhood than she believed, she thought she had been playing piquet nigh as long as he. Her father had taught her to play for comfits when she had been seven, and at the age of eleven she had fleeced her first pigeon—a young Portuguese nobleman who had thought it amusing to play for money against a boy. He had learned differently soon enough. She had the mental advantage then, for her opponent had thought her age made her a less challenging match. She was an adult now, and Sir William was unlikely to relax his guard because of her lesser age, though she hoped he thought it gave him an edge. But her sex? Now that was a different matter. She had found that men customarily believed women had no head for cards. She thought that this inability signalled a lack of opportunity, rather than an inborn lack of talent, but God forbid she should explain that. And God grant it would give her an advantage now.

She dealt, and again the cards fell in favor of Sir William, but not enough that she couldn't take the advantage at any time. Her blood was surging in her veins, and while she would never have hoped for it, in a way she welcomed playing from behind. Sir William's face was like stone, but there was a flaring light in his eyes that told her he thought he had won.

It was her deal again, and she was forced to admit to herself that he damn near had won. They were playing to a hundred points and he had seventy-four. She had fifty-seven, and the way the cards had been running she thought she had little chance of making her hundred before he did. She thought of the pistol in her pocket; she might easily need it yet.

She dealt, and felt a flare of excitement run through her. This was the hand she had been waiting for. She wouldn't gain much in the calling, but she thought she might possibly win most of the tricks.

She won them all, and laid down the last trick with a tight, triumphant smile. Now she would see whether he was a man of his word.

"Capoted, Sir William," she said quietly.

The look on his face was a mixture of astonishment and, surprisingly, admiration. She could see him quickly and professionally tallying the points in his head, and realizing that with the forty points for the capot added to points for the tricks she had won, she had made her hundred with ease.

"You're very cool," he said.

"I've had to learn to be," Catherine replied.

"I've never met a woman quite like you."

She paused, considering. "I suppose there aren't many who've had to be the way I am. I don't know that most would consider it a recommendation."

He looked at her assessingly. "If I have to be beaten, I think I prefer it be by someone of your caliber. It even makes me feel slightly less foolish about the affair with the Duchess of Tyne. You're a worthy opponent, Miss Catherine Brown."

Despite her best intentions, Catherine's breath caught in her throat. She had not dared to hope until this moment. She had been convinced she would have to resort to the pistol yet, and with that bring on her ultimate failure in England. But she thought now that Sir William meant to keep his word.

She allowed herself to smile slightly. "Does that mean that you'll keep your side of the bargain, Sir William?" she asked.

He frowned slightly. "Are you implying that I wouldn't? If you were a man—" He broke off. "I suppose you've been brought up in a different school than I, my dear. An English gentleman always keeps his word." He smiled wryly. "Even if it's my last act as an English gentleman. I suppose I'll be off to Venice now to join Marc Antonio."

"Well, give Marc Antonio my regards," said Catherine wryly. She had never liked the Venetian gambler much, and his latest act had certainly made life rather difficult for her.

Sir William apparently didn't hear the note of irony in her voice, for he nodded. "I will." Improbably, he added, "I think I find I'm proud to have known you." His lips twisted. "I'll be joining your numbers now, you know. Marc Antonio invited me long ago to be his partner, and I find now that I have no choice."

Catherine laughed. Her sense of relief was making her feel a little light-headed, she thought. "It's not such a bad life," she said. "You might find you enjoyed it. And if my opinion matters to you, I can tell you that you're like to be a success. I've never played a more challenging game of cards in my life. Although of course the stakes were very high."

"Thank you," said Sir William gravely. He walked across to his desk and scrawled a few lines, sanded the paper, and folded it. He held it out to Catherine. "This is a letter to my man of business, explaining that urgent affairs have made it necessary for me to sell Meysey Manor to you for certain private considerations. I doubt he'll be much surprised. It's not the first time I've done this sort of thing."

Catherine made no move to take the paper. The whole affair was starting to take on the overtones of some wild dream.

"Well, take it," Sir William said impatiently.

"It doesn't seem fair," Catherine said. "I never meant to strip you of your last possession."

"I stopped caring about the old place years ago. Take it,"

he said. "It frees me of all ties with England. It's better so, I think."

Catherine took the note and pocketed it. The man had, in his own strange way, a definite code of honour. She had in her life met men who were worse than he. "Thank you, Sir William," she said gravely.

"I'll show you out," he said. "It's best you go now."

He opened the door, and bowed in a courtly fashion to let her through. She inclined her head graciously, but they did not speak again.

Catherine never remembered too much of the journey back to Portman Square. She remembered flagging down a hackney, and sinking gratefully onto the seat. She found she was suffering extremely from reaction to her earlier fright. Jane opened the door to the house herself, but Catherine was barely able to form a coherent sentence.

"I think it's best I go to bed," she said, and crumpled in a faint on the floor. She sat up again almost immediately, much ashamed.

Jane hustled her upstairs, and put her to bed with a hot brick and a cup of tea. "You'll feel better in the morning," she said soothingly.

Catherine laughed. "Oh, Jane, you're so gorgeously sane in an insane world. You say the same thing for my adventures that you said for little Sophie's megrims."

"It works," Jane pointed out placidly.

Catherine's head was already sinking inexorably into the pillow. "Yes, it works," she said sleepily.

When Catherine opened her eyes the next morning, it was with a shake of the head, as if waking from a nightmare. How had she let one man's warm brown eyes alter twenty-seven years of training? She had let her scruples regarding Alec Carrock throw her into a morass of indecision from which she had only just escaped with her adventure still intact, the adventure on which not only she but

Richard and Jane as well, depended. It had taken the challenge of fighting Sir William to make her realize just how low she had almost sunk.

With a jump, Catherine cleared the bedclothes and, running to the window, threw open the curtains. The sun was shining and the birds were singing in the trees at the center of Portman Square. It was nearly the end of May, and she had let almost three weeks go by doing nothing. The Season would be over before they knew it.

Too impatient to wait for her abigail, she dressed herself hastily and ran downstairs. Jane was sitting in the breakfast parlor, ruminatively munching toast and sipping tea.

"It's high time I sent for Papa," Catherine announced as she walked in.

Jane dropped a piece of buttered toast onto her novel in her surprise.

"I can't imagine why I've been dawdling so long. Papa must be getting quite restive in Calais. He was never one to like sitting still. Although he *has* always liked French women."

Jane found little to dispute in either statement, and if she had her own views on Catherine's dawdling, she did not communicate them.

Catherine sat down at the table and poured herself a cup of tea. She considered it broodingly, as if she could read in the stray tea leaves the future of her plans. "I'll write a note this morning."

She sent a letter to her father, who was staying with a friend in Calais. Jean-Luc's seafaring enterprises had suffered since the peace, but he still maintained a wide net of dubious operations, which made communications with him easy. Richard should not come himself, she wrote, but should send Pedro with a letter, and Catherine described in some detail what that letter should say. Pedro was not to come immediately to the house, but was to stay at an inn and send a message.

All she had to do now was wait for events to occur, but

she did so with a renewed zest for life. The indecision she had felt had been deadly, she realized now, not just for herself but for Jane and Richard as well. Years ago—at her birth, in fact—her path in life had been set out for her. The world was a cutthroat, hard-scrabble place for those not born to a name and a competency, and she could not afford to indulge in foolish megrims. She had been reading too many novels, she decided cynically.

She cultivated her relationship with the dowager duchess once more, annoyed with herself for having allowed it to lapse. It was inevitable that it would have suffered slightly during the crisis with Sophie, but the dowager was a sensible woman who knew which side her bread was buttered on. She could not like anybody interfering in her affairs, and she may have even felt secretly daunted at the idea of a successor bolstered by the newfound security of loving and being loved, but she also knew that even the Verlains would have found it hard to survive the scandal that must inevitably have ensued upon the wife of the duke eloping with another man.

The dowager's manner towards Catherine initially possessed a hint of austerity, but she made no reference at any time to any part of the debacle, and as soon as Catherine made the effort to renew the relationship, it became clear that in the absence of Sophie, the old woman craved young female companionship. The relationship between Catherine and the dowager became, if anything, closer than it had before.

And with that intimacy, of course, came contact with Alec, which Catherine treated with a light hand and a sure touch, as if he had been only the premier of a field of avid cicisbeos. If sometimes she noticed a look of bewildered pain in his eyes when she flirted with him as charmingly as she knew how, she made sure to ignore it. And Alec himself seemed to fall quickly back into the role he knew best how to fill: the charming but unapproachable grandson of the Dowager Duchess of Tyne.

* * *

On a balmy evening in June, the message from Pedro came, and Catherine sat down, chin in hands, to plan the next stage of her plot. In pursuance of the conclusions she came to, she invited the dowager duchess to sup a dish of tea. With her, the dowager brought Alec, and if Catherine was slightly daunted by the thought of having to carry out such an involved deception beneath the eyes of a man who had once praised her honesty, she showed no signs, but poured tea with a steady hand.

At exactly twenty-five minutes after four o'clock there was a commotion in the hall. Catherine, the perfect hostess, made no sign of having heard, but Jane looked up with a frown.

"So unlike Bagwell to allow such a disturbance," she murmured under her breath. "I will go see what's wrong."

Catherine looked across at Alec, and saw a faint smile at the back of his eyes. Was he remembering, as she suddenly had, the morning he had disturbed Bagwell himself by demanding entrance? Her lips curled softly at the memory, and she saw an arrested look, as if something had pleased him, leap to his eyes.

But there was no time for such matters, for Jane was ushering Pedro into the room.

"Caterina, my dear," she said with a slight quaver in her voice, for she could act a part as well as any of them when she had to. "Look who it is."

Catherine set her teacup down on the table beside her with a visibly shaking hand.

"Pietro!" she cried.

Pedro, who was also known as Pietro or Pierre or anything else that seemed expedient, hurried across the room.

"*Marchesa*, *bellissima donna*," he cried, and continued in a stream of Italian.

Catherine jumped to her feet and grabbed his shoulders, replying in equally fluent Italian. She broke off and turned to her guests.

"I am sorry," she said brokenly, her Italian accent suddenly strongly evident. "Pietro is my father's manservant. He has bad news, I think."

She turned back to Pedro and cross-questioned him in Italian. He shrugged his shoulders and produced a letter. Catherine started to tear it open, then hesitated and looked to her guests.

"I am sorry. May I?"

"Oh, but of course," said the dowager, the sparkling eyes in her wrinkled face avid with interest.

Alec said nothing, but Catherine chose to ignore him. He was, at this moment, unimportant. She looked down again to her task of opening the letter, then spread the sheets out and started to read.

Slowly, gracefully, she sank into the chair she had been sitting in, her face turning white in delicate stages. After a minute she looked up and cross-questioned Pedro sharply in Italian.

He replied soothingly, and her colour returned somewhat. Finally, she looked at her guests, smoothing the sheets of the letter absent-mindedly on her knee.

"I am so sorry," she repeated again. "You must long for an explanation."

"Oh, no, my dear," said the dowager instantly, but it was clear that the exact opposite was true. Her curiosity was almost tearing her apart.

"It is my father," Catherine said. "I must explain, I suppose, that I have not been strictly honest with you. I know the English government supports the Austrian control of Venice, but I think many of you English do not agree."

There was enthusiasm in the dowager's eyes as she drank in Catherine's words. She nodded her head in agreement.

"I must tell you now," Catherine explained, "that my father is a patriot. He is one of those who has schemed for the restoration of Venice's sovereignty. But we knew it was dangerous. He sent me here to London because he became afraid for me if something should happen."

She raised a hand to her eye and wiped away a small tear. "Dear man, always he cares for me, but for himself there is never a thought. I begged and begged that he should come with me, but he said he must finish the last details of certain plans he had put in motion. Then he would come and join me in London."

She paused dramatically. The dowager hung upon her words.

"But he has been betrayed. He has been found out by the Austrians. He had to flee our palazzo with nothing but the clothes on his back and our faithful servant Pietro. He has had to go carefully, incognito, but he has sent Pietro on ahead to bear the news. Pietro assures me that he is unhurt, but there is still danger. I can only pray until he reaches asylum here in London." She looked down at her hands, lying calmly in her lap, with only the occasional nervous twitch showing her distress.

"Oh, my dear," cried the duchess. "How very exciting. What a sensation it will make. Our government may have to say they side with the Austrians, but everyone knows that England has always been the bastion and home of freedom. England will welcome your father with open arms."

Catherine blinked back a tear, and exulted silently. Her schemes were working exactly as she had contrived them; there were few greater thrills in life, she thought. The dowager would tell all of London, and soon her father would be welcomed back to his homeland as a hero. Richard was right, she thought triumphantly, this was the grandest hoax they had ever perpetrated.

And then she looked over at Alec, sitting silently a little past the dowager. He had a look on his face, not of suspicion—she thought he believed her story completely—but rather of distaste, as if he hadn't liked the scene she acted. As if there had been something in her manner that for him had rung hollow. She thought she knew what was bothering him. Her dramatic scene today had been quintessential Marchesa di Carabas. The marchesa was an affected woman, with a charming mask of flirtatiousness that many men found irresistable. Catherine had been fool enough to let that mask drop a little with Alec, and he had for a while believed that he liked the woman beneath that mask. He didn't like the resumption of her artificial ways; he thought he preferred the honesty he believed he had seen beneath. Well, he had never truly known the woman she really was, despite what he thought, for to know her would have been to know Catherine Brown. And that she had never been able to allow him to guess. If she were ever to reveal her reality to him—which of course she could never do—then she would truly see him turn from her in repulsion. For Catherine Brown had deceived Alec Carrock far more thoroughly than the Marchesa di Carabas, for all her artificial, flirtatious ways, had ever done.

Catherine sighed, knowing this would be in character with the part she was playing today, and the dowager was immediately all concern.

"My dear," she said, "you must want to be alone to assimilate this terrible news. We will leave you now." Her eyes gleamed, and Catherine knew she could hardly wait to spread this news. It would be the gossip of the *ton* within the day.

She smiled inwardly, and made her adieus to the dowager and Alec with a most touching look of distress on her face. And despite the unhappiness that it seemed meeting Alec must cause her, she forced herself to remember that she had just won a major battle for her father and Jane.

12

RICHARD BROWN ARRIVED on a lovely June day, when the early summer sunlight shone gently through the tender green leaves on the trees in Portman Square, and the birds sang cheerily. A slightly dilapidated hackney pulled up in front of the house, and Richard, slim, grey-haired, impeccably dressed, sprang out.

"*Caterina*," he called out before the door to the house had even opened. "*Mi Caterina*! *Figlia*!"

Bagwell opened the door, but before he had a chance to descend the steps, Catherine burst through behind him, and, like a bird taking wing, flew down the short flight and into Richard's arms.

"Father, oh, Father," she murmured in Italian. "How I have missed you. But now you have come."

He hugged her close wordlessly.

Both were so practiced at their years of deception that they could convey genuine emotions to each other without the slightest betrayal to an audience. Bagwell would be able to report to his household—and presumably from there the news would move to most of the other households of the *ton*—that the marchesa and her father had greeted each other most touchingly.

Catherine had withdrawn herself from Richard's arms and was leading him up the steps, talking to him of nothing much in a low, intimate whisper all the while. Now she knew, she thought triumphantly. Nothing had ever really mattered to her but Richard. Her interlude with Alec

Carrock had been a bad dream, born of distance from her father. Here, with Richard, was where life meant her to be. Surely the well-being and happiness she felt now, when measured against the distress she had felt when she believed herself in love with Alec Carrock, showed her that.

Ricardo Brinetti, Marchese di Carabas, was an immediate hit in London. The English always loved a romantic story, and in the Marquis of Carabas they found one made to order. He was the underdog, a patriot, a freedom-fighter, a man struggling for the kind of liberty the English prized so in his own country. The fact that their own government was theoretically allied with the opposing side disturbed them not a whit. They had been charmed by his lovely daughter for the past months, now they were delighted to take the father to their hearts.

It was soon discovered that the Marquis had managed to bring almost nothing with him in his flight from Venice. As he said, spreading his hands out expressively in that Italian manner so reminiscent of his daughter, "I was in peril of my life. I had ten minutes warning before the Austrian soldiers would be searching my palazzo. I took with me one clean shirt. Imagine that, a scion of the di Carabasi with only two shirts." He laughed good-humoredly, clearly a man far too secure in his own high-born lineage to worry about such matters.

Immediately Society rallied round to help him. Tailors, hatmakers, glovemakers were recommended to him, and of course those illustrious tradesmen were informed by their patrons that they would extend credit to the poor, exiled Marquis of Carabas. The tradesmen might wonder whether the poor, exiled marquis had brought with him the wherewithal to pay his bills, but this was not a matter that concerned the aristocracy, and the tradesmen knew better than to offend their entire influential clientele; it was better to chance a loss on this one man.

As soon as the marquis was properly outfitted he became

the hit of all Society. He was nominated to every club, from Boodle's to Watier's to White's, and made frequent appearances not just at every ball, musicale, and ridotto, but also at that sanctum sanctorum, that Holy of Holies, Almack's, where he was the darling of every lady from seventeen to seventy. The Dowager Duchess of Tyne, especially, he wound around his little finger.

Privately, he congratulated Catherine. "You have performed impeccably, *cara.* You are a true daughter of mine. The Dowager Duchess of Tyne, no less. She is still as much the Queen of Society as she was when I last, unlamented, left these shores. A wonderful choice."

Catherine smiled gently, but did not respond as exuberantly as might be expected. Now that the first joy of her reunion with her father was over, she was finding that her life was not as settled as she had believed. Alec Carrock's face still occasionally haunted her dreams, and she would sit bolt upright in her bed at nights, still sweating from a nightmare in which he had discovered all and confronted her in wrath.

She loved her father still, but was finding there were places in her life he could not fill. She thought she had sensed that even before she left Venice, but now she knew it. There was a part of her that longed for a stability, an end to lies . . . and a family of her own. That longed for more than that, that longed for Alec Carrock.

She found to her great distress that her father was more perceptive than she had believed. Somehow—she didn't know if perhaps Jane had betrayed her, or whether there was still something in both hers and Alec Carrock's faces when they were together—he had discovered that the man had an interest in her, and he had a way she was starting to find most annoying of reminding her of it.

"It would be perfect, Cat," he said plaintively one morning at breakfast. "Think of it. The man's fabulously wealthy, we're supposed to have lost most of ours since I fled Venice. He need not know how much we never had."

"It would be lying," Catherine said.

Richard's face fell. "Oh, no, Cat. Not lying. It's a trick, a grand scheme, the perfect plot."

"It would be lying," Catherine said flatly.

Richard was not a fool. He knew when to retreat, and he said nothing more that morning, but he developed an unpleasant habit of trying to throw Catherine and Alec together. It was not as easy as it might have been, for Alec was clearly avoiding Catherine, but Richard and the dowager were charmed by each other, and willy-nilly their two descendants were occasionally thrown together.

Richard had accepted an invitation to a small afternoon soirée at the house of Miss Mary Fielding. Miss Fielding was an anomaly that London society had accepted on the grounds of her extreme wealth and impeccable lineage. A lady who by now must be well into her fifth decade of life, she possessed neither striking good looks nor a fashionable manner, and apparently no wish to marry, for her fortune was such that she could have been a veritable antidote and still found a husband. And she was by no means an antidote. She had straight, pale brown hair fading slowly into grey, which she wore pulled back into a neat chignon at the back of her neck, and a pale, bony face that was actually growing more lovely as she aged. But she showed no interest in attracting, and despite her fabulous fortune, dressed plainly, almost Quakerishly in simple dresses of grey or brown.

She was known to have an intellect, and her parties often had something of a literary style to them, although she never distressed her acquaintances in the *ton* by making this too marked, and Scott or Shelley were more likely to be the order of the day than deeper philosophers.

Today, when Catherine and Richard appeared, the subject at hand was Byron, for this poet was still considered the epitome of scandalous behavior. His wife had left him the previous year, and it was now widely known in England that he had fathered a daughter on Claire Clairmont some months previously. These scandalous tidbits only added a lustre of wickedness to the projected appearance of a new book of poetry, to be called *Manfred*, in the next few weeks.

As Catherine and Richard were greeted and sat down, Catherine noted with distress that the dowager and Alec Carrock formed one of the number. She wished that if she was going to foreswear the man she could do so in a decent, complete way. She wondered with annoyance if Richard had known that he was likely to be there when he had insisted on making an appearance.

But she had little time for such reflection, for Miss Fielding's companion Amelia Dunsany, a happily widowed dumpling of a woman some years Miss Fielding's elder, looked up with excitement.

"But of course, here we have someone who knows whereof Byron speaks. My dear Marquis, when I see you, I cannot help but think of those immortal lines from *The Prisoner of Chillon*."

And she stood to declaim in a low, dramatic voice.

> "Eternal spirit of the chainless Mind!
> Brightest in dungeons, Liberty! thou art:
> For there thy habitation is the heart—
> The heart which love of thee alone can bind;
> And when thy sons to fetters are consigned—
> To fetters and the damp vault's dayless gloom,
> Their country conquers with their martyrdom,
> And Freedom's fame finds wings on every wind."

She sank to her seat, quite overcome with the drama of her performance, but had soon recovered her breath.

"Oh, Marquis," she squeaked, "whenever I look at you I think of that. That you could have been mouldering in some dungeon. . . ."

She continued to speak, but Catherine's attention was caught by a quietly closing door. The dowager was still seated in the room, but Alec Carrock had apparently just left. She thought the action was in some way a comment on herself, although she did not completely understand it, but even within the limits of their occasional meetings Alec had been growing colder and more withdrawn to her as the weeks went by. She had wanted to discourage him, but she had not asked for hatred. Or had she? Oh, sometimes she wished she were as sophisticated and worldly-wise at love as she appeared. She wished that every scathing glance he threw her way didn't hurt so much. She wished she understood.

Mrs. Dunsany was still burbling away gently in the background, and after some moments Catherine looked up to see a quiet smile of ironic amusement, as if they knew something no one else did, being exchanged by Richard and Miss Fielding. The sense of complicity there surprised Catherine. Miss Fielding was not Richard's normal kind of flirt.

Outside the door, Alec Carrock leaned against the wall of the hall attempting to control a surging anger he could not even try to explain. It had overwhelmed him so completely he had felt forced to leave the room until he could control himself, and he had mumbled some excuse to his grandmother and hastily left.

This . . . this adulation of the Marquis of Carabas, and by extension his daughter, left him feeling almost physically sick. Where was the Caterina that he thought he had been coming to know? Buried completely under a pile of artificiality and falseness such as he had never seen the like. Oh, why had he believed that she was different? She had betrayed him as completely as every woman eventually did. More so, for he had trusted her. What a fool he was! He took deep, panting breaths of air, trying to calm himself, and after a while the sickness started to recede, but it was a long while before he felt able to return to the room.

* * *

June was nearing its end, and the Season too was drawing to a close. To Catherine, used to the heat of countries like Italy and Spain, the weather still seemed mild, but the *ton* was complaining of wilting in the heat and talking longingly of Brighton or their country homes. Richard, after having posted out to the Cotswolds to see Meysey Manor and deciding it was quite habitable, announced he was organizing a house party there. Catherine, although unsure exactly where his schemes were leading them, was acquiescent.

When he invited the dowager and Alec Carrock to attend, she smiled brightly. Only afterwards did she remonstrate with her father. By then of course it was useless, the invitation was out, and all her objections accomplished were to cause Richard to look at her with hurt on his face.

"But, Cat," he pleaded. "You know we agreed to come to England to get you married."

"I never agreed to it," she said. "At least not with Mr. Carrock."

For once Richard gave up his argument. He looked down at her with a tender expression on his face.

"I want you to marry for your own good," he said. "I would never force you into something you didn't want."

"Oh, Papa," she murmured, embracing him. "Have I ruined all your plans? I know this is what we came to England for. I'm so sorry."

Surprisingly, he laughed a little, an odd expression on his face. "Well, I wouldn't say you've ruined all my plans. At least, not yet."

But he, who was usually so open with his schemes was not any more forthcoming. "I don't know yet," he said with unwonted modesty and a look of doubt on his face. "I may be mistaken. We'll have to see."

Catherine forbore to press him. She knew now what it was like to have a secret or two.

* * *

Alec had no intention of going to the Carabases' house party, but had not wanted to offend his grandmother by committing them publicly, so had remained silent. Several days later, however, she decided to accept another invitation, one to stay with friends in Brighton. She had been an intimate of the Prince Regent in her younger days, and still maintained a fondness for him.

"And since I have been abandoned by my grandchildren," she said pathetically, "what else is there for me to do?"

"Balderdash," said Alec firmly, refusing to be manipulated. "Anyway, Sophie just wrote you yesterday to say that she and Tony will be returning for your final ball."

"But then they're going to Anthony's hunting box for the summer," she said with an annoyed sniff. "Of all the ridiculous starts. There's not room for me there."

"Has it occurred to you, ma'am," Alec said unsympathetically, for he was finding his patience with his grandmother was not as great as it used to be, "that that may have been exactly what they had in mind?"

The dowager had the grace to grin at him. "I'm sure it is. And I have to say I think more highly of the two of them for it. Your Uncle Joseph and Aunt Maria never had such gumption. It's all the fault of that di Carabas chit, of course."

Alec changed the subject.

Sophie and Tony returned on a breathless June afternoon, and Sophie promptly flung herself out of the chaise and into Alec's arms.

"Darling Alec, I'm been thinking all the way down of you. You must take me for one of our drives in the park so I can thank you properly."

Alec looked down at Valancourt, who was chewing the tassel on his Hessian boot.

"Only if you promise not to bring that repellent creature with you."

With a cry Sophie swooped down. "Oh, Val," she said, grabbing the little dog and tapping his nose with one finger. "You naughty, naughty, sweet little dog."

Tony grinned. "Discipline, as you can see, is a trifle lax with my wife and her pet," he informed Alec. "I've been trying to teach her a little about training dogs, but it doesn't seem to have taken."

Sophie pouted adorably. "Tony, you don't mean that at all," she scolded. "Poor Val is far too little to be trained like your big rough dogs."

Tony smiled tenderly. "I'm afraid I don't have the heart to discipline him properly. I'm far too grateful for his influence with you regarding Sir William."

Sophie giggled.

The drive in the park was taken the following afternoon, and if Alec had had any doubts about the success of his and Caterina's meddling, they were laid totally to rest.

Sophie was absolutely, deliriously happy.

"And Alec," she said, leaning over confidentially, "I'm increasing. Isn't that wonderful? Can you imagine me a mother? Or Tony a father, for that matter? But you mustn't say anything yet, because Tony still hasn't decided how best to tell Grandmother."

"Oh, she'll be pleased," Alec said with confidence. "He'll be the heir to the Duchy of Tyne, after all."

"What if he's a girl?" pointed out Sophie.

"Then you'll just have to try again," Alec said with a straight face. "Not an unpleasant task, I gather."

Sophie giggled, and didn't reply. After a minute she sobered.

"I went to see Caterina this morning," she said. "I don't think she's very happy." She peeped up at Alec under her eyelashes, assessing his reaction.

Alec's face was set hard. "I don't see that much of her any more," he said.

"Yes, I gathered that. Why not? I rather thought you

liked her. I don't know why you shouldn't. She's quite my dearest friend."

Alec scowled out over his horses' heads. "Did you never notice she was just amusing herself with us?"

Sophie's wide eyes showed her surprise. "No. Oh, Alec, I don't think that's fair at all. Why, I owe everything to her! And to you too, of course. What makes you say that?"

"She said it herself. She's like most women, a flirt and a lying socialite. She'd sooner jump off a bridge than tell you the truth."

Sophie scanned his set face with worried eyes. Dimly, she understood that Alec, whom she had always considered the paragon of all virtues, was in a great deal of pain. Up in Northumberland with Tony, deliriously in love herself, she had conceived the notion that maybe Alec had a little bit of a tendre for her dear Caterina, and she had rejoiced at the thought. She had brought up the subject of Alec with Caterina, and it had been received in much the same chilling way that the subject of Caterina was being received by Alec.

She wasn't sure what she should do, but she longed to make things right.

"I don't think that's fair, Alec," she repeated steadfastly. "I like Caterina a lot, and have always done so. She has a very kind heart, and was incredibly good to me. I think you're wronging her."

He glanced down at her. "Do you think so, little Sophie?"

"Yes," she said firmly. "I do."

He drove on without replying for some time, and she was wise enough to say nothing.

Finally, he broke the silence with a faint smile. "Is this tit for tat, Sophie? I insist on solving your romantic problems, so you interfere in mine?"

"I greatly appreciate what you did for me, Alec," she said stubbornly, "and what Caterina did as well. I think you're wronging her. I may not be very bright, you know, but I know a good person when I see one, and Caterina is one. She was kind to me. I don't believe she's what you say."

Alec thought about that. For weeks now, he had lived in a slough of misery over Caterina. Just the sight of her was enough to cast a shadow over his day, and he was unable to tell why he should have let her get under his skin in such a way. She mystified him. He had thought he was getting to know her, that there was someone there who was admirable, even lovable. He had rejoiced in the apparent honesty of her manner, in the direct gaze of her green eyes when she was enjoying herself. And then, just when he had thought he had found a woman unlike any other he knew, she had retreated back behind a mask of flirtatiousness and artificiality. The pain of realizing how mistaken he had been in her had been the greatest of his life, even greater than the childhood betrayal of his father's death.

And yet Sophie had seen the same woman he had, and believed that woman really existed. Did she? he wondered. Was there a real person there behind the beautiful mask?

He looked down at Sophie. She regarded him with eyes full of doubt, as if wondering whether he had taken offense at her plain speaking. He smiled encouragingly, and immediately a smile sprang back on her face.

"So you think I'm wrong, do you?" he said wonderingly. Sophie's sureness of belief was strangely catching. "What should I do about it?"

"Give her another chance, Alec. Sometimes I think you don't like London Society all that much. Maybe she doesn't either."

Alec laughed scornfully. "She? Why she's the perfect Society lady. What makes you say that, Soph?"

"I don't know. Things she says sometimes. Give her a chance, Alec. Go with her to this house party the marquis is talking about."

"Do you think she wants me to?

"I don't know. Yes and no. Maybe. She acts just like you, Alec. All confused."

He scowled. "Confused? I'm not confused."

Sophie retreated hastily. "Oh, no, Alec. I'm not sure I really meant that."

They drove on in moody silence, broken after a while by Sophie.

"Will you go, Alec?"

He looked at her with exasperation on his face. "You're not going to let up until I agree, are you?"

"No," said Sophie simply.

"Well, all right, then," said Alec ungraciously, wondering why he had capitulated. And yet . . . and yet . . . there had been something in Sophie's words that had given him new hope.

13

It was in the end a small group that left London for Meysey Manor, and Catherine was surprised to see few of the bucks with easy money to lose at gambling, or the rich widows of easy virtue whom Richard normally preferred to associate with. There were several men of middle age whom Richard had met at the various clubs he had joined, but the centerpiece of the party was the very correct Miss Mary Fielding, who had also brought her cousin Mrs. Dunsany. Since Richard's tastes normally tended towards women of more voluptuous charms, such as the richly-endowed Signora della Lucca had been, Catherine was doubly surprised.

Meysey Manor was a long, low house built in mellow Cotswold stone during the reign of Elizabeth. While not as grand as many later buildings, especially those of the last century, it was possessed of a certain charm that appealed immediately to Catherine. It was hard to reconcile such a house with the gambling, hard-living Sir William. She wondered if that was why he had shown little affection for the place.

The servants appeared pleased by the change of masters. Apparently Sir William had made only the occasional appearance during the hunting season, and they were happy to have some activity in the house. Catherine had insisted that Richard use almost the last of their savings to pay the wages, and this had been a popular move. It seemed that Sir William had been a little erratic concerning this matter in the last few years.

Catherine had spent the days before their departure from London in agony. When she had taken the initiative to cut off the intimacy between herself and Alec Carrock, it had never occurred to her that there might come a time when she would live in the same house as him, would have to see him on a daily basis. Considering his coldness of late, she was extremely surprised that he would have seen fit to accept the invitation, and could only wonder why he had. The disturbing thought took root in her mind that he had only done so to distress her. She could not think it of him, and yet there seemed no other explanation.

Most of the party had gone out to Meysey Manor on a Saturday, but since the Dowager Duchess of Tyne had not made plans to leave for Brighton until the Monday, and she insisted Alec remain with her until her departure, he would be joining them on the afternoon of that day. Catherine looked forward to his arrival with a great deal of trepidation, and found she was having difficulty sleeping.

Monday afternoon was hot, and most of the house party enjoyed thinly, or not so thinly, disguised naps. Catherine was far too nervous to indulge in any such thing, and only she and Mary Fielding remained awake. They sat in what had been the solar of the Elizabethan manor, and now had been made into a most charming ladies' parlor, Catherine with a book, Miss Fielding with some embroidery. After some while, Miss Fielding looked up to catch Catherine staring fixedly out the window.

"It's far too lovely a day to stay immured in here," she said. "Will you take a stroll around the garden with me?"

Catherine jumped slightly. "I'm sorry. I was thinking of something else," she explained. "I would love to go outside."

They linked arms and strolled in quiet companionship across the lawn and down towards the stream that ran at the edge of the little wood. Mary Fielding was a restful person to be with, Catherine discovered. She did not attempt to make conversation when none was wanted. Catherine wished that her own thoughts could be as calm as Miss Fielding's appeared to be, but she was dreading Alec's imminent appearance. She thought of making an excuse to return inside but skulking in the drawing room seemed futile when she would have to meet him eventually.

By the time they heard the crunch of wheels on the gravel carriage drive, Catherine had worked herself up into a state of nervous anticipation so great she thought she must surely scream. What would he say to her when they saw each other once again? What would he do?

Mary looked across the wide stretch of lawn at the phaeton bowling up the carriage drive. "Ah, that must be Alec Carrock now. I'm pleased the marquis invited him. I haven't seen much of him of late, but his father was my mother's cousin. He was a sweet little boy. I used to visit them at Carrock House occasionally, but after his mother moved back to Tyne I never saw much of him until he was old enough to come to London. It will be nice to see more of him here." She started to move across the grass towards the drive, and Catherine was forced to walk with her.

She would have given anything to have run and hidden at that moment, but she had little choice in the matter. Miss Fielding would have found it very odd if she had done so. But she found she was dreading Alec's inevitable icy glare.

Alec had had a wonderful drive down from London. The sun had been out, the wind scooting little puff ball clouds across the sky, and the roads dry. The greys had been eager and willing for the first stage, and the horses on each successive change had been good ones. In all, it had been a pleasant drive, and he had found himself strangely eager to see Caterina. Maybe Sophie was right. Could he have been so mistaken in her? Perhaps now, in new surroundings, they could make a fresh start and find again that joining of kindred spirits that he had once been so sure he sensed in her. He found he was forgetting the image of the flirtatious Society woman that had distressed him so, and remembering the eager girl who had driven his phaeton so splendidly, the intense friend who had schemed with him to save Sophie.

So when he drove up the carriageway at Meysey Manor and saw her distant figure walking across the lawn with Mary Fielding, he forgot the past weeks enough to wave cheerfully and uninhibitedly. Pulling up the horses, he waited for Jemmy to jump down and go to their heads, then vaulted from the phaeton himself.

"Mary," he called when they had approached. "I'm glad to see you down here. How have you been keeping yourself since I saw you last?"

"Well, enough, Cousin Alec," she said, presenting her cheek. "I'm glad you came, even if your grandmother was unable to do so. I think you'll find it very lovely here. And here is the marchesa waiting to greet you."

The inevitable moment had come. He turned from Mary to find Caterina regarding him unblinkingly. She stood tall and graceful, with her hands held calmly at her sides, yet there was, of all things, a trace of fear in her cool green eyes.

"Alec," she said, holding out her hand.

He grasped it, and felt it icy despite the heat of the day. There were emotions there he had never sensed before. He wondered what they were.

"Caterina," he said warmly.

Something flared in her eyes that seemed to be delight. Or was it merely relief? She smiled, and there was a genuine warmth there. He knew now that he hadn't imagined that. There was something between them.

"Welcome to Meysey Manor," she said quietly.

The party soon developed a quiet rhythm of its own. During the day the older gentlemen and ladies usually strolled in the gardens, for the weather was extremely fine, and Richard almost always seemed to pair off with Miss Fielding. Alec and Catherine, as the only members of the party under forty, were constantly thrown together.

Catherine knew in her heart of hearts that she should try to avoid this, that she should not be encouraging Alec Carrock in any way. But she couldn't resist the temptation, and so she walked and talked with him as eagerly and as openly as she had when she first met him.

And in the sweet, gentle, sunny summer days, they discovered that the newfound peace and harmony of their meeting on the carriage drive had not been a mirage. They possessed a mutual interest in many matters that surprised both. At first, inevitably, there were moments when both were stiff and intolerant, but the slow pace of the country infused them, and they came to find that with the hustle and the bustle of the London Season behind them, they could share time in simple happiness.

Catherine had never fished before, but Alec was apparently an enthusiast, so she spent hours on a bank under a willow tree with him, watching him cast his line with boyish glee, and eventually venturing to join him in the sport. She had spent so much of her time in mannish pursuits that she had far more talent for the sport than might have been supposed, at least by Alec, who had known her mostly as the jewel-bedecked denizen of London ballrooms.

At nights, alone in her bedroom, Catherine would ruminate on the situation, and knew it couldn't last. She had lied to Alec Carrock about almost everything in her life. What would he care that in one important matter, that she had lost her heart to him, she had always told the truth? Honesty was important to him, he had said, and she was the least honest of women. She was a gambler, a trickster, an adventurer. She thought that if matters had been different he might have fallen in love with her as she had with him, but life had not given her that. All that life had given her was permission to enjoy him for a few short weeks here and now.

And sighing, leaning her elbow on the window sill and watching the peaceful, moonlit English fields beyond the gardens, she would wonder how she could ever go back to her wandering life when this was all over.

But the days were hers to enjoy, and in an almost frantic fashion she was enjoying them. She had told herself some weeks ago that she was born to be an adventurer, and she would never be anything else, but here at Meysey Manor she realized that she could never be one in England. She hated to call it quits on anything, but she would on this. As soon as the summer was over, she would marshal her father and Jane and Pedro and they would go back to Europe. It was a pity to have spent all this money on this enterprise for nothing, but they had been broke before, and undoubtedly would be broke again. Nearly six months outside the various countries of Europe where they were best known would have given them a breathing space. They could go to Paris or Rome or Madrid, and resume their old ways.

For the next few weeks she would forget all that, and just enjoy the company of Alec Carrock, because soon enough she would lose it. That decision made, she found she could put off the persona of the marchesa, and be herself again. And when she did so, she found that Alec came back to her, and she saw the old light of admiration spring up in his eyes once more. But the guilt no longer consumed her, for she knew now that she would leave him in just a few weeks. There could be no harm in enjoying being with him for just a little while . . . if she would be gone before anything could come of it.

And so they walked in the gardens, and fished, and drove Alec's phaeton through the narrow lanes surrounding the manor. And most of all they rode together, for Sir William had left several quite adequate hunters eating their heads off in the stables. Here, Catherine was in her element. For her, even the feel of a smooth pair of carriage horses obeying her commands had never matched the feel of a spirited horse plunging across a meadow and over a hedge. She wished she could ride astride, for riding side-saddle she could never match the communion with her mount she felt while riding astride, but even side-saddle would do, with Alec at her side.

One morning early, before breakfast so they could catch the cool of the day, they took the horses out and raced an arranged steeplechase course over the meadows, hedges, and ditches of Meysey Manor. Alec was a bruising rider, and the chestnut he bestrode was a fine Irish-bred hunter, but Catherine seemed powered by an inner flame. From the moment that Alec called "Go" she shot forward on the black thoroughbred mare she had made her own.

Leaning far forward to give the mare as much speed as possible, she had drawn in deep breaths of the crisp English morning and known that this was where she truly belonged. She guided her through the first field and over the first hedge, then pushed on at a neck-or-nothing gallop that left Alec several necks behind as they maintained a blistering pace. Seeing the second fence, a cut-and-laid hedge with a ditch in front, she sat down in the saddle and steadied the mare, feeling her tug eagerly at the bit.

"Easy, girl, easy," she murmured, "this one can't be taken so fast."

She risked a glimpse behind her, and saw Alec pounding up, his face alight with an enthusiasm to match her own, but they were fast approaching the fence and she needed all her concentration on the jump. Holding the mare steady, she let her out at the last second and cried out with joy as they easily sailed over the jump, which had to top four feet.

A herd of cows scattered at their approach in the next field, but Catherine was unaware of anything except the thrill of the speed and a good horse beneath her. Alec never had a chance to match her, but the end of the race was a pull up a slight hill, and the mare, tiring, faltered a little. The bigger chestnut pulled up beside her, and they finished the course almost neck-and-neck, but with Alec a definite head behind.

Catherine let out an uninhibited whoop of glee before springing off to let the mare breathe. Alec jumped down next to her, and companionably side by side they walked their sweating horses across the breezy hilltop.

"I won," Catherine exulted. "I beat you by a head!"

Alec looked at her. He smiled, and seemed about to say something, then changed his mind.

She was quick to catch his mood. "What were you going to say?"

"I was thinking how different you seem," he said. "I can't reconcile you with the woman I thought you were in London at all. More like the one I drove back from Richmond, or the one who badgered me into rescuing Sophie. I had come to think I was mistaken, that you were only interested in balls and such."

She looked away, hiding her face momentarily against the mare's neck.

"There's more to life than balls," she said finally.

"I think I could be happy if I never went to another one," he said.

"I dream sometimes," Catherine said quietly, "of a cottage in the country where I could live very happily and quietly. I like England, you know. Jane always spoke to me of it with such love and longing that I grew up always dreaming of it. I think that Jane and I could find a little cottage and live alone there together."

His tone matched hers in dreamy seriousness. "I think sometimes of moving to the country and farming my own land, as my father did. He was a wealthy man, you know, just as I am, and yet he never bothered himself with London Seasons or fashion. I was eight when he died, and I have very few memories of him, but I do have one. He had taken me out into the hills to see all the shepherds who cared for the flocks. He must have had twenty or thirty flocks, each with their own shepherd, scattered across the fells, and of course he had an estate agent, but he cared enough to check them each himself. And I remember the sunshine and the wind on those bare hills, and he and I together with a nuncheon in a saddle bag. I think he must have died very shortly after."

"And that was when you went to live with your grandmother?" Catherine asked.

"Yes," he said, looking out over the gentle rise and fall of the Cotswolds.

"Do you ever think, then, of giving everything up? You could be a—what is it called—a gentleman farmer like your father, couldn't you? Why don't you?"

"My grandmother would never forgive me," he said.

"As would my father, if I went to live in that cottage with Jane," she replied. "But sometimes I still dream."

In silence, but in mutual agreement, they turned and walked the horses down the hill and back towards the manor house.

Time continued to flow with the same dreamy happiness, but Catherine knew that there was now some intensity in hers and Alec's relationship that had not been there before. She knew that if she had any sense she would put a stop to it, she knew she was only courting future unhappiness, but she couldn't seem to help herself. That same defiant voice that had tempted her into kissing Alec in Vauxhall Gardens now told her that she should seize happiness while she could. And so she let it go.

The climax came upon her suddenly. If she had had more experience in such matters, if she had seen it coming, perhaps she would have done something to head it off. But she was naive when it came to matters of the heart, and she didn't.

It had been another hot, dreamy day, and they had spent the afternoon fishing under the willow. It was just past midsummer now, and in the long English evenings dusk came very late. Despite the fashionable London hour of seven that Richard insisted on keeping for dinner even in the country, the last golden rays of the sun were still falling across the garden when the party rose from dinner.

Alec stood at the French windows that overlooked the flagstoned terrace, and when Catherine joined him he turned to her.

"Will you join me in a walk?" he said. "It's far too lovely an evening to waste indoors."

She smiled, and took his arm, and they strolled across the golden, sun-warmed Cotswold flagstones of the terrace and down the steps flanked by pillars topped with stone balls and onto the lawn. Across the lawn, behind a manicured yew hedge, was the rose garden, and with slow, intimate steps they headed there.

The hedge had over the years been trimmed so that it formed an archway that gave access to the rose garden. With the general neglect under Sir William, it had become a little ragged, but the gardener had been spurred by the renewed attention and it had now regained its past perfection.

Catherine paused and looked up at it. "The entrance to an enchanted garden," she said. "I have always thought that of arches in hedges."

Alec said nothing, but laid his free hand where her hand rested on his arm.

They passed through the arch and into the garden, where the roses were just coming into bloom, their sweet perfume scenting the air. At the end of the walk was a stone bench, and they walked towards it, the hem of Catherine's dress whispering lightly over the grass of the path between the roses.

They sat down, and watched the last, lingering rays of the sun gild the many colors of the roses.

"Do you remember the daffodils?" Alec asked in a low voice. "It seems so long ago now."

Catherine felt as if she were in a dream. "A long, long time."

He put his arm around her, and she did not resist. It felt so warm, so right. She turned her face up to his as naturally as a flower does to the sun.

He lowered his head, and tasted her lips with his.

She shifted, but only to draw closer.

His lips were moving over hers, and she knew that this was right. That this was the most perfect thing that had ever happened in her life.

She sighed.

Their kiss deepened.

They were linked together by something more than physical intimacy. She thought there would never be a moment happier.

And then somehow, without her knowing how, she was bowed under the force of his embrace, pressed back almost to the sun-warmed stone of the bench. She could feel his hands warm and firm on her back through the paper-thin silk of her dress, as his lips wandered down her neck towards the rise of her breasts, exposed by her evening gown.

He tasted the sun-touched skin there, and she felt her nipples peak and grow taut. A fire leaped and exploded inside her. Her own hands, which had been linked behind his neck, of their own volition started to explore the muscles of his back, hidden though they were by his coat.

She whimpered. It wasn't fair. There were so few clothes on her, so many on him.

She struggled slightly, and he let her free. With trembling hands she undid the buttons on his coat and wrapped her arms inside, but even that was not enough. She pulled the shirt loose, and ran her fingers up and down the heated skin of his back.

He gathered her into his lap, and she felt the intensity of his desire. A formless longing was gathering inside her. He lowered his head once again, and kissed her on the lips, a long, deep-drawn kiss of longing and passion.

And then he stopped.

She sighed, and surfaced as if from under water, shaking her head slightly.

"Caterina," he said. "Cat, my little Cat. Will you marry me?"

The words were a drenching spray of cold water.

She gasped in shock, and looked up at him with fright-filled eyes.

"No," she said. "No, I didn't mean that at all."

It was his turn for shock to fill his eyes. "No?"

"I didn't mean to lead you on. Please absolve me of that," she said incoherently.

"You won't marry me?"

"No. I mean I don't know. Oh, Alec, forgive me."

He slid to his knees in front of her, heedless of the damp of the grass. "Caterina, what are you talking about? I love you. You love me, don't you? I thought you did. You seemed to."

"Oh, Alec." She couldn't help the words. "Yes, I love you."

"Then marry me."

"I can't."

"Why not?"

She slipped from his grasp and ran from the garden. He, burdened with the need to tuck his shirt back in and rearrange his coat before returning to view, was unable to follow for several minutes. When he emerged through the arch, she had nearly reached the house, and as he watched she ran in through the French windows and escaped from his sight.

The moon was shining down across the rose garden, which Catherine could see from the window of her bedroom. She sat, her head resting on one hand, pondering the very meaning of her life. And she knew, above all, two things. That Alec would never forgive her if she told him. And that she would never forgive herself if she didn't. She also knew that she could no longer live the life of an adventurer. Perhaps in a year or two, maybe even a few months, she would be able to, but just now her heart was too tender.

She had to escape. She had to leave now. She couldn't face Alec again. There was no answer she could give him.

Sighing, she picked up her candle from the table beside her bed. Lighting it at the candle left burning in the hall, she padded towards Jane's door in her nightshift and bare feet.

Jane, woken from a sound sleep, was Jane. Calm, comforting, the perfect mother. She had a solution.

"You'll go to my friend Dylys in Cumberland," she said calmly. "She owns a millinery shop there. Perhaps she needs an assistant, and certainly you have always had a talent in that direction, my dear."

Catherine smiled briefly, thinking of the score of hats she had trimmed this Season alone.

"Yes," she said.

"If she doesn't," Jane said, "maybe she'll know someone who does. At the very least, she'll keep you for a few weeks for my sake while I think of something better.

"We'll send you in the gig to town at dawn. You can catch the stage into London, and the Night Mail north tomorrow night. I would come with you, but I think someone needs to stay and explain to your father."

Catherine laughed, although there was still a break in her voice. "I'm not a fragile English flower, am I, Jane? I can cope with a stagecoach on my own, I think. I'll take my pistol just in case, but I doubt there will be much need."

She packed one bag, light enough to carry herself, with a few dresses and necessities, and just before five Jane went down to the stables herself and rousted up a sleepy stable boy to harness up the gig and drive Catherine into Cirencester.

And as she left, Catherine turned around one last time, to see the sleepy Elizabethan manor dreaming in the first rays of the morning sun. Somewhere, asleep in a room upstairs, was Alec. She would never see him again.

Upstairs, Alec pounded the pillow and then placed it firmly over his head. By the time he had reached the drawing room the evening before, Catherine had disappeared to her room. If he were not to make a scene, there was nothing he could do. She clearly didn't want to talk to him that night, so he had submitted gracefully. But come morning, he swore, he would have it out of her. She loved him, she had told him that. Why then couldn't she just marry him? It was generally what was done, he believed. Loyalty to her father? Perhaps. Alec had found the gentleman as charming as everybody did, but there was a certain air of disingenuity about him that annoyed him, especially when fools like Amelia Dunsany were burbling on about his patriotism. Alec had not thought that patriotism rang very true. But that didn't mean he wouldn't be willing to take the old man to his bosom too if that were necessary. But there had been real fear in his Caterina's eyes. What was wrong?

He removed the pillow from his head. It didn't seem to help. He tried putting it under his stomach and burying his nose in the mattress. That didn't help either. At least another two hours until he could decently get up. Another four before he could decently confront Caterina.

He threw the pillow across the room.

14

THE TOWN OF Keswick, in Cumberland, is a charming place, all grey stone houses and narrow cobbled streets leading down to the shining blue lake that is Derwentwater. About three blocks up from the water, on the right, is the shop of Madame LeBlanc, Milliner. And on a hot day in late July, with the breeze blowing off the lake providing the only coolness, a gentleman left his phaeton at the main coaching inn and inquired the way to Madame LeBlanc's shop.

The shop had a bow window and a small, inviting green door. With a crash, the gentleman flung the door open. There was a violent tinkle of small brass bells above his head. The lady sitting behind the counter, whose head was bent over a bonnet to which she was painstakingly adding feathers, looked up with a start.

Upon seeing the gentleman, she dropped the bonnet. Her hand went to her breast, as if to cover her heart.

"Alec," she whispered.

"Yes, Alec," he said. "And a damn time I've had of it too, tracking you down. How dare you just disappear on me like that?" he asked threateningly.

"You don't understand," she said in a low voice.

"Oh, don't I? I think I do, Miss Catherine Brown."

"I suppose you would have to know," she said despairingly, "if you have found me here. Did Jane tell you?"

"Yes, and egged on by her, your father contributed his mite."

"I knew you would be angry," she said. "I can't blame you. That's why I left."

"I'm only angry that you wouldn't tell me. Oh, Catherine." His voice shook a little. "Catherine, why did you run away like that? Didn't you know it wasn't the initial deception that mattered, but only that you couldn't trust me enough to tell me?"

She looked down fixedly at the floor, then jumped off the stool and kneeled to retrieve the fallen bonnet.

He came around the counter and took her shoulders in his hands, speaking to her bent back. "Catherine, I love you. I told you that. I still love you. I love everything about you, but most of all I love that essential honesty in you. That honesty that would not let you deceive me. That honesty I saw shining out of your eyes from the very beginning."

"I'm done nothing but trick people all my life," she said to the floor. "I'm a gambler, an adventuress."

"And yet you would not lie to me. I offered you my hand and fortune, yet you would not take it because you dared not tell me the truth. Do you know how few women there are in London of whom I could say the same?"

"No," said her muffled voice.

"If there's one in a hundred," he said, "I'd be surprised." He shook her shoulders insistently. "Catherine, Catherine, look at me."

And finally she raised her face, to reveal green eyes gleaming with tears.

He put his hands, one on either side of her face, and looked her in the eyes.

And at that moment the shop bell tinkled to announce another customer coming through the door.

"Damn," said Alec, and let go of Catherine.

The old lady who had entered looked scandalized, though whether at his embrace or his language could not be certain.

Madame LeBlanc, or Miss Dylys White as she had been

known when she was Jane's childhood friend, came hurrying out from the back of the shop.

"Catherine, do you need help here?" she called. She stopped and stared openly at Alec.

Alec bowed. "Madame, I am kidnapping your assistant," he said. "I'll return her in a few hours."

Dylys had heard something from Catherine of what had spurred her sudden arrival, and perhaps she had overheard a little from the back as well.

She smiled. "That would be fine, Mr. Carrock. I assume I *am* talking to Mr. Carrock. I shall wait on Mrs. Hardaway."

Mrs. Hardaway sniffed, but Alec paid no attention. He whisked Catherine out of the shop and up the street.

"Where are we going?" she asked breathlessly.

"Out of the village. There's a nice private lane with a view of the lake. Very romantic."

"How do you know?" she asked.

He gazed down at her fondly. "My little dear. Did you not know you were running away into my own back garden?"

"What do you mean?"

"Did I never tell you where my estate was. It's here. Barely ten miles away. Keswick is our market town."

Her face flamed. "No!"

"Yes."

"Oh dear," she said inadequately.

He laughed. "And this from the lady who single-handedly fooled all of London. Not to mention my redoubtable grandmother."

She turned away. "I didn't think," she murmured. "I was too upset."

They had reached the edge of town, and turned into the little lane he was speaking of.

He put his arm around her shoulders and drew her to him. "Oh, Catherine," he said, "what am I going to do with you?"

She looked up at him with wide, unblinking, honest eyes. "I don't know," she said. "What do you want to do with me?"

He walked her to a gate in the hedge and leaned against it, looking down at the lake below them. She climbed on the gate and perched atop it, her long slim legs dangling. He put his arm around her again.

"Catherine," he said.

"Yes?"

"I'm going to ask you one more time. Will you marry me?"

Catherine looked down at the top of his curly head. "If that's really what you want," she said.

"That's good," he replied, "I would have hated to drag you to the altar."

They were silent for a few moments. Below them, the sun glinted on the lake, while overhead the curlews called.

Finally Catherine stirred. "I can't believe how accepting I'm being," she said, with wonder in her voice. "I don't know anything."

"Do you want to hear?"

"If you want to tell me."

There was silence. The wind whispered through the hawthorn hedge.

"I almost didn't understand," he said in a low voice. "When I found you'd left, I was so angry. I persuaded myself once again that I had been mistaken in you, that you were everything I had once accused you of. A typical, silly, artificial woman. I didn't know why you'd left me the way you did, but I think I just thought it typical of women."

She sighed. "I knew that," she murmured. "I knew you would hate me. But what else could I have done?"

"You could have told me."

"Would you have listened?"

He stared out across the lake. "I don't know. No."

"So what happened then?"

"I went back to London, but nobody was there. I thought of going down to Brighton to join my grandmother, but I couldn't stand the thought. I thought of joining Tony and Sophie in the Shires, but I would have been incredibly *de trop*. And everywhere I looked, I saw your face. I didn't sleep much at night. I tried drinking, but it's never helped much. I boxed a bit with Jackson, took my horses out, but nothing seemed to give me sleep. So I ended up thinking a lot."

"And?"

"And I realized that nothing I knew about you made sense." He was speaking in a low rapid voice. "That the only thing I knew for certain was that when you looked at me full in the face, I believed in you. That you were the only woman I could ever love, and that nothing else about you made sense."

A slight sniffle came from Catherine. Alec ignored it.

"So I realized that there had to be a missing clue. Unless I was mad, there had to be something I didn't know that made you sometimes act the way you did. But I hadn't the faintest notion what it was."

Catherine gave a slightly watery laugh. "Well, it's good to know how well I did my job. So what happened then?"

"Well, actually it was your father. Once, when we were at Meysey Manor, late at night, when he had drunk a little much, he made a remark that didn't make much sense. I don't think anybody really noticed—he recovered fast enough. We were talking one time of the caverns in the Peak District, and he mentioned that a boyhood friend had broken a leg there. I think I must have looked inquiring, because he immediately said that he had spent one summer in England as a boy. But I was surprised, even so. You had told me of your mother's connection with England, but had never said anything of your father."

Catherine blushed fierily. "That was all a lie," she muttered.

"But with what grace you pulled it off," he said. "I'm sure I would never have guessed if I hadn't fallen in love."

She ducked her head, and stared fixedly at the ground.

"Anyway," he said. "I also wondered about you and Sir William Meysey. It seemed odd that he would have sold his home to you, of all people. I was willing to accept it, for the man obviously needed money, but I wondered."

"You were, I suppose the only one who would," she said. "I didn't think of that."

"I hadn't thought much about it at the time," he admitted. "But it was just one more piece that didn't seem to fit. And no matter how I tried, I couldn't make the pieces fit. So in the end, I went back to Meysey Manor, and appealed to Miss Verne."

"She always liked you," Catherine admitted.

"You wouldn't have thought so to see the way she stared me down," he said. "You would have thought I was a robber come to steal her most precious treasure. It took me forever to convince her that I really loved you, and would love you no matter what. Eventually she broke down and told me."

"And?" Catherine asked. There was a tinge of fear in her voice.

"I don't think I have ever met a braver woman in my life," he said.

"Brave?" she cried. "But I deceived you."

"But I don't think you ever did it for a love of deception," he said. "If you had, you would have married me. There was no need to tell me. You had me besotted; you could have wound me around your little finger if you had even tried. Your father says he begged you to. Yet you didn't."

"I couldn't," she said. "I tried to think I could, because I owed it to my father, but I couldn't."

"No, you couldn't. That's what I mean. Every woman I've ever known—even Sophie, dearly though I love her—gets her way through such little deceits. Half the women in London lied to the men they married in one way or the other. Yet you, with so much more at stake, weren't willing to."

"No," she said, "it wouldn't have been right."

He raised his head to look at her, and for the first time since he had begun his story she gazed straight at him. Her green eyes were clear and luminous.

"I only did what I had to do," she said.

He clenched his hands on the top rail of the gate. "You have no idea, do you? You are the woman I didn't believe existed. How will I ever convince you of that?"

Catherine didn't answer. She found that a lump seemed to have formed in her throat that made speaking impossible.

He took her by the shoulders and swung her down from the gate, as easily as if she were a feather.

"I think I'm just going to have to kiss you," he said.

She looked up at him, remembering the night at Vauxhall, when they had stood looking at each other in just such a way. His classically sculpted face was just as handsome still, yet he was so much, much more to her now. It was as if all the agony had a purpose, as if it had melded their love into something far finer than that first passion.

She smiled.

He lowered his head, and his lips took hers.

Hours, days, aeons later they drew apart.

"Catherine," he said. "I'm going to ask you one last time, now that all explanations have been made. And this time it must be what you want, with no doubts or questions in your mind. Catherine Brown, will you marry me?"

All doubt had left her eyes. " 'From this day forward,' " she quoted softly, " 'for better for worse, for richer for poorer, in sickness and in health, to love and to cherish.' Oh, Alec, I do love you."

Leaning together against the gate, they stared out over the lake once again.

"It's so lovely here," Catherine breathed. "I wish I never

had to leave. If I hadn't been so desperate over losing you, I would have been happy here."

"I stayed at Carrock House last night," he said. "It's been closed up for over twenty years—I only stayed in a couple of rooms when I came up—but I think we could bring it back to life. Would you do that with me? Shall we stay up here and farm sheep together?"

She turned and looked at him. "Alec," she said. "Would you do that? Give up London altogether. What would your grandmother say?"

"My grandmother," he said, "can go to—"

He caught himself.

Catherine grinned. "I've heard far worse, you know. The denizens of gambling dens don't often watch their language."

"My grandmother can take care of herself," he said austerely. "I've given her over twenty years of my life. It's Tony's turn. I'm going to raise sheep, as my father did before me. And you're going to raise them with me. No more gambling dens for you, Catherine. If I ever catch you near a deck of cards—" He paused. "When I think of you taking on that blighter William Meysey, my blood runs cold."

Catherine reflected that it was possibly a good thing she hadn't told Jane the whole. There were, upon reflection, certain things it was better one's future husband not know. Honesty did, after all, have its limits.

"I hate to raise this question," she said, "but what about my father? I can't consign him to the nether regions, Alec," she said with anxiety in her voice. "I'm the only one he has, my dear."

Alec grinned. "I forgot to tell you one detail."

"What?" said Catherine.

"Well, when I returned to Meysey Manor, I walked in on a celebration. Apparently your father is going to marry Miss Mary Fielding."

"What!" cried Catherine in outrage. "That slipped your mind?"

"I had more important matters to think of."

She shook him. "How dare you? I can't believe it. Papa . . . married . . . to Miss Fielding. Alec, you're having me on." She quieted down. "And yet . . . ?"

"And yet," he said. "I think Meysey Manor must be an extremely romantic place. I did notice a few solitary walks were being taken by your father and Mary."

"There was something," she said, considering. "She's not his type. I noticed that immediately. That should have made me suspicious. But Alec, it's terrible. I know my father. He'll marry her without a qualm about his secrets."

"And I know Mary," Alec said. "She told you, didn't she, that she's my cousin—second cousin, to be accurate, but I'm known her for years. She's one of the most astute ladies I have ever seen. She sits there so quietly, you don't realize she's observing you, until you look up and surprise a gleam in her eye. There are few people who can fool Mary."

Catherine thought about this. She remembered the gleam she had surprised in Mary's eye that afternoon in London.

"If Mary's not figured out the whole by now, I'd be very surprised," Alec said. "Believe me, your father hasn't half the skill you have. She's guessed."

"Oh," said Catherine.

"So you see, the new marchesa will take care of your father. And of course—I won't even make you ask it—we will have Jane with us. But now for the most important question. Miss Brown, will you raise sheep with me for the rest of your wedded life?"

"With all my heart," she said, leaning up against him. "Will I like sheep?"

"Yes," he said positively.

She brooded on the subject. "Could we raise children as well, do you think?"

"They're trickier than sheep," he said.
"Yes, but brighter."
"You may have a point there."
He looked down at her, and a gleam came to his eyes. "They're also more fun to create," he said with a wicked leer.
Catherine laughed, and leaned against him.
"When can we start?"

AUTHOR'S NOTE

I HAVE ALWAYS loved fairy tales, almost as much as I love Regencies, so when Mary Elizabeth Allen of Walker suggested to me that I might like to write a Regency based on a fairy tale, I leapt at the notion.

But what to do? "Cinderella" was my first thought, but it seemed too obvious. After all, isn't the classic Regency novel about a poor but beautiful girl who goes to a ball and meets a handsome prince? I wanted to find something a little more special. And somewhere along the line, the idea of "Puss in Boots" came to me. It's always been one of my favorite stories, and (like most people, I suspect) I've never had many doubts that the cat, not the miller's son, is the hero of the piece.

So what, I suddenly wondered, would happen if I made the cat into the *heroine* of the story? And what about if I changed the princess (who was the reward in the story) into a prince and gave my cat the reward she so clearly deserved. By this point, ideas were coming fast and furious. I filled the role of the miller's son—who would play the pretend marquis—with the heroine's roguish father, and cast as the king of the country that classic of Regencies, the terrible old mother or grandmother who rules her family—and frequently Society—with an iron fist.

I have to admit that I didn't stick too closely to the plot. There were too many characters in my story that were calling to be set free. The princess in the fairy tale is a complete non-entity, which clearly Alec Carrock could never be allowed to remain. And the story of Sophie and Tony is, of course, completely the product of my imagination. But I feel that the central theme of the "Puss in Boots" tale, the one that has appealed to readers for generations, is the story of a born trickster playing the ultimate hoax on the establishment. So that is what I have tried to bring out in my story.

In the original tale, the cat asks his master for a pair of boots, and then goes off to the King to plant the idea in the King's mind that the Marquis of Carabas is somebody that the King should admire and look forward to meeting. In illustrations of the tale, the cat is almost always shown very handsomely dressed, frequently in a feathered hat and a cape as well as boots. So I made sure that Catherine had made a stop in Paris to outfit herself (even if the jewels were paste) before she arrived in London.

After the King has been made aware of the existence of the Marquis of Carabas, the cat then plots a way in which the two can meet. In the original, the marquis has supposedly been bathing in a river when robbers steal his clothes. This, of course, disguises the fact that the miller's son is not dressed the way a marquis should be. In my version, I used the fact that Northern Italy—and Venice in particular—had just fallen under the rule of the Austrians, to suggest a variant on robbers. If the putative marquis had been forced to flee for his life, then he, as in the original tale, could not reasonably be expected to produce the standard trappings of rank and privilege.

The final trial of the "Puss in Boots" tale is an ogre that the cat must vanquish. In typical fashion, the cat does this, not by brute force, but by trickery. The cat goes to visit the ogre, and mentions to this fearsome creature that he has heard that the ogre can transform himself into all sorts of creatures. With his typical ingenuity, the cat persuades the ogre to change himself into a mouse, and then eats him up.

My ogre was, of course, Sir William Meysey, who has

been terrorizing the local populace (i.e., Sophie) and tries to confront the heroine with the traditional fate worse than death. Since my Catherine was an experienced card-sharp, I wanted the duel of wits to involve a card game. I chose piquet because it is always played by just two people, and because Georgette Heyer's duplicitous heroine Prudence, in Heyer's classic story *The Masqueraders*, also plays piquet. It wasn't until I came to write that scene that I realized that I, who have never won a game of poker in my life because I am totally unable to master the whys and wherefores of the odds and the betting, had locked myself into writing about something that makes poker look like a game for four-year-olds! Luckily Catherine has a better head for cards than I do, and won the match handily.

The grand finale of the story portrays the King so impressed by the grandeur and obvious wealth of the ogre's castle, which the cat says belongs to the Marquis of Carabas, that he gives his daughter's hand in marriage to the marquis. My version is, I hope, less materially practical and more romantic, for it shows Alec and Catherine finally—almost—falling in love in the idyllic setting of Meysey Manor in the Cotswolds.

I hope that *The Marquis of Carabas* has been as fun to read as it was to write, and that the fairy tale angle added an extra dimension to your pleasure. If it did, then I have succeeded in my purpose in writing this book.

Elizabeth Brodnax
May 1990

If you would like to receive details of other Walker Regency Romances, please write to:

The Regency Editor
Walker and Company
720 Fifth Avenue
New York, NY 10019